T0319132

Unleash your heart...

Young features editor Eugenia Shaw is thrilled to have a scoop on not one but two major stories for *Lady Fair* magazine. The last thing Gena expects is to fall in love—with a quirky looking Chinese Crested named Wiley. Or with the fellow Crested lover she keeps accidentally-on-purpose running into in Central Park...

Unlike Gena's ambitious and self-centered live-in boyfriend, Paul is a man who appreciates Wiley's unconventional elegance. And the better they get to know each other, the more it appears that he appreciates Gena, too. Soon she can't help noticing how much happier and more confident she is when they're together. She's even beginning to see a new Gena when she looks in the mirror. But will she be brave enough to rewrite her own next chapter?...

Books by J. M. Bronston

A PURRFECT ROMANCE

HER WINNING WAYS

SUMMER ON THE CAPE

A COWBOY'S LOVE

WHO DO YOU LOVE?

Published by Kensington Publishing Corporation

Who Do You Love?

J. M. Bronston

LYRICAL SHINE
Kensington Publishing Corp.
www.kensingtonbooks.com

LYRICAL SHINE BOOKS are published by

Kensington Publishing Corp.
119 West 40th Street
New York, NY 10018

All Kensington titles, imprints, and distributed lines are available at special quantity discounts for bulk purchases for sales promotion, premiums, fund-raising, educational, or institutional use.

Special book excerpts or customized printings can also be created to fit specific needs. For details, write or phone the office of the Kensington Sales Manager: Kensington Publishing Corp., 119 West 40th Street, New York, NY 10018. Attn. Sales Department. Phone: 1-800-221-2647.

Lyrical Shine and Lyrical Shine logo Reg. U.S. Pat. & TM Off.

First Electronic Edition: December 2017
eISBN-13: 978-1-5161-0320-1
eISBN-10: 1-5161-0320-3

First Print Edition: December 2017
ISBN-13: 978-1-5161-0321-8
ISBN-10: 1-5161-0321-1

Printed in the United States of America

Acknowledgements

It's a pleasure to emerge from the solitary world inside which a book gets written, and give a thank you where it's due.

In the case of this book, I especially owe much to Anne-Marie Karash at the Humane Society of New York. I had many questions, and she was patient, sensitive, and generous in giving me her time and sharing information about the Society's mission specifically and the work of animal shelters generally.

While I hesitate to single out one of my precious daughters for special thanks, in this case I must acknowledge the invaluable help I had from Annie, on whose expertise I relied so frequently while writing this book.

To owners of Chinese Crested dogs all over the world, I thank you for your Facebook posts, from which I have gathered much of my understanding of these lovely dogs.

Most affectionately, I acknowledge our beloved Wiley and Piute (known as Pie), on whom much in this book is modeled, and their "brother" Bozzie. Also, Will Parker, Andy Schwalen, and Wendy and Bruce Kelly have been so important in their lives, and I hope they know how thankful we all are.

My agent, Liza Royce, is an unflagging fount of energy and support and I am so deeply thankful to have her and Ginger Harris and their whole literary "family" in my corner.

For his patience and support, I thank my editor, John Scognamilio, his team at Kensington Publishing, and most particularly Rebecca Cremonese who took the time not only to answer all my questions, but also to locate some very esoteric information for me. How lucky I have been.

And lastly, Mary and Margaret, I never forget you, even if this time your big sister gets a special thank you. Where would I be without all three of you?

Chapter One

Pouring rain. Middle of the night. Middle of the woods. Middle of goddamn nowhere. And now it felt like the car had a flat tire.

"Oh, damn!"

Nothing to do but get out and check.

Gena got a flashlight out of the glove compartment and slogged out into the mud.

And now this! Already hours late getting back to the city. Warren will be pissed. I'll never hear the end of it.

She'd tried to call him after she left the cabin, but the place was so remote she couldn't get a cell phone connection. She knew she shouldn't have stayed as long as she did, but the woman had been so interesting, and her work so beautiful, she just got totally caught up in the interview and by the time she had everything she needed, it was already dark.

It's my own fault. I get so wrapped up in what I'm doing...

She shined the light on the front left tire. Looked okay. With a steadying hand on the car's hood, she got around to the tire on the right, and there didn't seem to be a problem there either. By now she was totally drenched; the water was running down the back of her neck into the collar of her blazer. Her brand new Jimmy Choos were ruined and her pants were all muddied. "Oh, *Lady Fair,*" she said out loud. "What I go through for you."

To keep from sliding in the mud, she had to hold on to the car doors as she got herself to the back of the car. Right rear tire looked okay. And, to her relief, so did the rear left tire.

Well, whatever it was, thank God I don't have to be changing a tire in this mess.

Now all she had to do was get herself back to the highway and find a service station. At least she'd be able to call Warren and tell him not to worry. He'd be mad about her delay in getting back, but she could worry about that later. Now she just wanted to get out of the wet. Slipping and sliding, she got to the door, got hold of the handle, and pulled it open. But she didn't get into the car right away. Because, through the racketing noise of the downpour through the trees, she heard something else. It was a kind of whimpering sound, high-pitched and urgent.

She paused. Gena was a city girl. Being alone in a dark forest was a little too much like being in a Grimm's fairy tale. A whimpering sound in the night was not something she wanted to investigate. Especially when she was hours late getting home, in a pouring rain, with her clothes all ruined and sodden trees looming scary all around her.

But she also had been born with a powerful curiosity gene. It's what had been getting her into trouble ever since she was a kid—and it was also what had made her a journalist. And maybe some little creature was in trouble. Gena was also a tender-hearted girl, which had also often gotten her into trouble. Even now, she didn't stop to think that maybe it was a rabid raccoon or a bad-tempered coyote or an injured fox, something ready to bite whoever came too close.

She shined the light into the trees, along the mucky ground, and there, only steps away, was a small dog, half buried under drooping shrubbery and huddled up against a jutting tree root. In the flashlight's beam it looked silvery, with sharp, pointy ears and a long pointy snout. The dog had no collar and was shivering miserably. And it was watching Gena with big brown eyes.

"Oh, you poor thing. You're in even more trouble than I am."

What could she do? Her jacket was already muddied, so she took it off as she ducked in among the branches, wrapped it around the dog, and lifted it out from under the dripping bushes. Back in the car, she put the dog on the seat next to her. It curled right up, facing her, with its eyes fastened on her as though it would talk to her.

"Well," Gena said as she used a tissue to wipe rainwater off her face, "you don't seem to know enough to come in out of the rain. Don't you have a home?" She pulled down the sun visor to look in the mirror and check the damage. Her long, blonde hair was soaked, matted around her face, and had bits of leaves stuck in it. "God, I'm a mess." She looked at the dog. "You don't look too great yourself. I'd take you home so they could clean you up, but I have no idea where home is." She hadn't seen a single house after she'd left the cabin, and that was miles back along the road.

There didn't seem to be any practical solution. "I think you're going to have to come with me. Maybe when we find a service station we can get us both cleaned up, and see if they have any ideas about what to do with you. And we'll get you something to eat. You look so skinny."

She started the engine, and as soon as they were in motion the dog laid its head down on its paws and got comfy. The car seemed to be okay, and Gena decided that what she'd thought was a flat tire was just the rutted road. "Maybe it was a divine providence," she said to the dog, "that made me stop right where we could find each other." The dog's ear was twitching, so Gena knew it was listening. "I think you should know," she said, "I'm not a dog person. There were no pets in my family. Dad was allergic and Mom was scared of animals. So don't even think you're coming home with me. Not that I wouldn't be willing. That is, I guess I would. But I know my boyfriend wouldn't agree to share our space with anyone. And if you think he'd be taking you out for walks or getting you to the vet when you're sick, forget it. Warren Haglund is not exactly the nurturing type."

The dog seemed unconcerned and was already doing what dogs do so well: it had closed its eyes and gone to sleep. It was apparently glad to be out of the rain. But Gena went on talking into the slapping of the windshield wipers, with the night and the rain out beyond.

"I never thought about it, really. But now that I am thinking about it, I know Warren would definitely not be wild with joy if I brought you home. He's not that kind of man. He likes his comfort. Long as I've known him, long as we've been together—well, I do know how he is. He'd look at you, all wet and skinny and hungry, and he'd say, 'You'd better find a home for that animal by morning, because we're not having it around here.'"

She felt embarrassed as she said it, like if the dog woke up and heard her, its feelings would be hurt.

"You are pretty pathetic looking. How long have you been out there, all alone, no food, all wet and homeless? Cold and lonely. Don't have a collar on you. Don't even have a name." The dog opened an eye and looked at her. "At least I should give you a name. Then you wouldn't be so pathetic." She glanced sideways. "And to think I was afraid you might be a coyote or a fox. Something dangerous. That's a laugh. But still, with that sharp nose and those pointy ears, I guess coyote wouldn't have been so far off. Like the cartoon guy, Wile E. Coyote. He's such a sad character, maybe a little bit like you? Are you a wily coyote?" She thought a moment while the wipers went *flip-flap, flip-flap*. "That's a good name for you. Wiley. That's it. That's your name. Wiley. I like that."

The dog's ears perked up and Gena decided the name was a success.

Half an hour later, out on the highway at last, she pulled onto the shoulder and got out her phone. Warren's message was short.

Where r u? Don't call

Going to bed now. U lost again?

"You'd think I make a habit of getting lost. Happened just once, just the one time. You'd think he'd get over it." Wiley pricked up his pointy ears. Gena smiled at him. "Warren can be very critical. Don't even get me started." Wiley was apparently a sympathetic, though silent, listener. "Okay, Wiley. Let's find a place where we can wash up and maybe get a sandwich or something. See if we can figure out what to do about you. Must be an all-night place open somewhere along the road."

It was almost two a.m. before the lights of a service station appeared. There was hot coffee, a couple of roast beef sandwiches, and a chance to gas up the car. There was also, unfortunately, an empty-headed kid behind the counter who was no help in finding Wiley's home. No, he said, there hadn't been anyone around asking about a lost dog. And no, he didn't know what to do about Wiley, but he sure wasn't going to let her leave the dog with him. Maybe she could wait till morning, he said, and go to the nearest town, Shanesville, and find a vet or someone who'd take him. Or she could post notices around the city. Put an ad in the local paper?

She got back into the car. Wiley was fully awake now, and watching her closely. Was she going to have to put him out into the downpour? She couldn't yet bring herself to do it. "At least I can see that you get some food first." She unwrapped one of the sandwiches and broke off a piece. She held it out to him and was surprised by how daintily he took it from her fingertips. "Someone taught you good manners," she said. She fed him the rest of the sandwich in pieces, then ate hers.

"And now, Wiley, the time has come." She lifted him out of the jacket and he stood up on the seat. Earlier, when she'd wrapped him up, drenched and shivering in the dark, she hadn't really had a good look at him. Now, uncovered, she really saw the dog she'd taken in out of the rain.

He was totally hairless! Absolutely the only hair on him was a bright tuft on his head, a set of unruly bangs that fell over his face. There was also a bit more at the end of his long, skinny tail, like a pale flag, and some more on his dainty paws. She'd never before seen a truly hairless animal, and he looked kind of spooky. His color was a beige so pale he was almost white, which explained why he had looked silvery in the light of her flashlight. His legs were very long for his small body and so skinny they looked breakable. He was as lean as a greyhound.

"I don't mean to hurt your feelings, Wiley," Gena said, "but you're a very odd looking animal." She stroked the soft hair on his head and rubbed his pointed ears. He rested his head in her hand and they looked into each other's eyes.

"I don't know what I'm going to do with you."

It was still raining hard, and she looked out into the downpour.

"I can't just put you outside here at this gas station, out in the rain and all alone, just hoping someone else would take you in. And that kid inside won't let you stay there."

There was nothing else to do.

"Tell you what, Wiley. You can come back to the city with me, and I'll take you to a shelter or the ASPCA or some place. They'll find a nice home for you."

She started up the car, and an hour later she was pulling into the parking garage of her building on East Seventy-Third Street. It was almost four in the morning, and she was dead tired but she had to give Wiley a couple of minutes to walk around the nearest tree. Then she carried him in her arms through the lobby, with a smile and a nod to Alfie, the night man on the desk, and up the elevator to the forty-first floor. She got herself quietly into the apartment, took a pillow from the sofa, put it down on the kitchen floor, and laid Wiley onto it. He was asleep in a couple of seconds. She took only a little bit more than that to get out of her clothes, wash her face, brush her teeth, and fall into bed and into a sound, sweet sleep.

Warren never even stirred.

Chapter Two

"What the hell is *that*?"

Warren was standing in the doorway of the bedroom, pointing into the kitchen.

Gena stuck her head out from under the blankets. She'd had only a couple hours' sleep, so she wasn't prepared to deal with Warren, not just yet.

"What's what?" she murmured.

"There's an animal in the kitchen. Some kind of dog, I think."

Her head was clearing, gradually. "It's a long story."

"Yeah. Well, I'd like to hear what he's doing in our kitchen."

"Give me a minute. I'm not awake yet." She stumbled into the bathroom.

He followed her, waiting impatiently outside the bathroom door. "I thought you went up to Connecticut to do a story on some artist up there. How'd you wind up with a dog?" His tone was definitely accusatory. Like he'd caught her again doing something dumb.

She came out, drying her face. "I found him in the woods," she said. "It was raining. Raining hard. I couldn't just leave him there."

"He doesn't even have a collar. Or a tag, or anything."

"I know. That's why I couldn't find his owner."

"So what were you planning to do with him?

"I'll take him to a shelter or something. They'll find a home for him."

"He's all muddy. Couldn't you have cleaned him up before you put him to bed on one of our pillows?"

"Warren, I'd been driving for hours. I was wet. I was tired. I was just glad to get home. And you were sleeping. I didn't want to wake you up."

"He doesn't have any hair on him. He looks weird."

"I know. I kind of like him."

"You would."

"Well, you won't have to look at him. I'll find a place for him."

"Where will you take him?"

"I don't know. The ASPCA maybe. Or the Humane Society. I'll find a place."

"Okay. In the meantime, could you clean him up a little? I don't want him dirtying up our stuff."

"Okay. Okay. I'll give him a lovely bath with suds and perfume and everything. Don't worry. He won't spoil our perfect home."

"Don't make that sarcastic face, honey. It doesn't look pretty." He pecked a small kiss on her mouth. "See you later. I've got a golf date."

Chapter Three

She didn't know much about animals. And Warren was pretty clear that he wasn't going to give Wiley one minute of his attention, so he was no help. And anyway, he'd gone to play golf with his boss, so Gena was on her own. But she knew enough to know Wiley needed to be walked. She could improvise a collar and a leash with some string, but that seemed so pathetic. Like a homeless person, holding up his pants with a piece of rope.

She carried Wiley down to the doorman's desk in the lobby. It was Saturday, so Seferino was on this morning. Sef was a sweet guy and she knew he'd help if he could.

"Sef, you sometimes walk dogs for people in this building. What are the chances you might have an extra collar and leash for this animal? I have to take him out and I don't have either."

"You have a dog now, Ms. Shaw? That's nice."

"He's homeless. I found him. He's just temporary."

"Let me look." He went into the package room, rummaged around for a minute, and appeared carrying a spare collar and leash. "Here you are, Ms. Shaw. Will this this do?"

"You're a peach, Sef." She slipped a couple of dollars into his hand. "You always come through. Thanks a bunch."

The day was lovely: sunny and warm, with just that teeny bit of soft breeze that makes you glad you're alive. And Gena was dressed perfectly for this perfect day. She'd left her long hair loose, and she was wearing comfy sandals and a little flowery sundress. "Warren doesn't approve of this dress," she said to Wiley as they walked out into the sunshine. "He says it's too short." It was true; Warren thought it was too short and that it didn't sufficiently conceal her "beanpole" legs. But Warren was off with his boss and she could wear what she liked.

She walked with Wiley in the park, basked in the glorious day, nodded to other dog owners out with their pets, smiled at the professional dog walkers with their multiple charges on multiple leashes. She discovered a population of New Yorkers she'd never noticed before, a population of dog-walking, dog-owning, dog-loving people, and she felt as though she had inadvertently joined a club, as though her identity had been expanded just by having Wiley with her.

"See, Wiley?" she said to him, pointing to a family out with a fluffy, frisky little white dog. "You can have hundreds of friends here in New York." She bought a hot dog from a vendor and sat down on a bench to eat it. She fed a bite to Wiley, who hadn't had any breakfast. "I usually put sauerkraut on my hot dogs, but I wasn't sure you'd like that." Wiley was silent on the subject, which showed her he was an excellent listener, the kind who pays close attention to every word and doesn't interrupt. On her way home, she bought a Good Humor ice cream and left enough on the stick for Wiley to finish. She wondered if ice cream and hot dogs were okay for dogs. "I hope I'm not making you sick," she said to him. He had those wonderful brown eyes fastened on her, and she was sure he was telling her he was okay, that ice cream and hot dogs were fine with him.

On East Seventy-Second Street, just west of Lexington Avenue, they passed a brownstone building with a bronze plaque beside the front door. *Funny*, Gena thought. *I've passed this building hundreds of times and never noticed this place before.* The plaque read:

AARON ZWEIG, D.V.M
VETERINARY MEDICINE
open 24 hours, every day

Wiley was sniffing around the iron railing in front of the entrance. "What do you think?" she asked him. "Maybe instead of the Humane Society or the ASPCA—?"

Wiley offered no objection.

"Okay, let's see what Dr. Zweig says."

Dr. Zweig turned out to be big and burly, like a large bear. About sixty-five, she judged, with kindly brown eyes, a graying beard, and an easy smile. He was wearing a white coat and escorting a woman with a cat in a carrier to the front door. There was no one else in the waiting room.

"Come in, come in," Dr. Zweig said, holding the door open for her. "My receptionist ran out for a few minutes, so it's just me. There's paperwork she'd give you, but you can do that when she gets back." He led her to an examining room. "So, who is this little guy?" He picked Wiley up and put him on the examining table.

"I call him Wiley. I brought him in because I'm not sure what I should do." She explained how she'd found him and said, "He had no collar or tag or anything, and I was thinking I'd take him to maybe the ASPCA, but we were just walking by and I thought maybe—well, I wasn't sure—" She paused and then added, "My boyfriend hates him. He thinks he's ugly."

"But you're thinking of keeping him?"

"Well, I don't know—"

"I'll just check him out. Sometimes owners have an electronic chip implanted so he can be identified."

"Oh, I guess we should do that." She practically bit her tongue saying it, hoping there'd be no chip.

Dr. Zweig reached behind him and took a small scanner from the drawer under a counter. "Takes just a moment," he said, and he held Wiley gently in place and passed the scanner over his back, between his shoulders, then around his shoulders and over the tops of his legs. "Nope," he said. "Nothing's showing up. So it's up to you. Have you decided? Are you going to keep this little guy?"

She looked at Wiley. And in that moment, she and Wiley came to a silent agreement.

"Oh, yes! Yes, of course. How could I not? Even if my boyfriend hates him. Even if he makes fun of him." She was feeling all fizzy inside. "Look at that sweet face. And he'd have died out there in the rain, so far from everything. He really would have, he was so cold and so skinny. Of course Wiley can have a home with me." She felt a thrill as she said those words, as though something important had just happened in her life.

"So what do I do now?"

In twenty minutes, Dr. Zweig had given him his shots, checked him all over for ticks, lumps, bumps, et cetera, pronounced him healthy, given her some brochures and explained her legal obligation to try to find the owner, and prepared to send her away happy. But not before he said, "Your boyfriend should learn something about this breed."

"This breed?"

"Oh, yes. You didn't know?" He was obviously surprised. "This dog you found is a classic Chinese Crested. Probably purebred. He wouldn't have had any trouble finding a home. Lots of people like them. They're sweet dogs. And very smart."

"But he looks so funny. So odd."

"That's an interesting thing about this breed. They often win ugly dog contests—such an injustice to the breed, I think, for they can also be very elegant. Look at him. Look at that sleek build, the long legs. The very erect ears." Dr. Zweig looked fondly at Wiley. Then, gently, as if to encourage her to be pleased with the dog's appearance, he said to Gena, "It's all in the eye of the beholder, isn't it?"

Chapter Four

She had her iPhone out as soon as she was back on the sidewalk, and she was Googling "Chinese Cresteds" as she walked Wiley to the corner and waited for the traffic light to change.

By the time it turned green, she'd learned about hairless Cresteds, like Wiley, and the Powderpuff variety, which are not hairless. By the time she reached the pet supply store on Lexington, a little boy had pointed at her and made fun of her "icky looking dog"; a woman stopped her to say, "My daughter has one just like yours, dear, and I think they're lovely, no matter what anyone says"; and a homeless man called to her from a doorway, "Does he speak Chinese?" At the pet supply store she bought a collar and a leash, a box of bright blue, environmentally friendly doggie poop bags, a couple of chew toys, a furry, stuffed, green-and-yellow-striped "snake," and a bag of specially prepared dried dog food. Also a book "all about" Chinese Cresteds. At the desk in her building, she returned the borrowed collar and leash to Seferino, and in the elevator on the way up, still Googling, she learned that Chinese Cresteds are not at all Chinese— maybe originally African, or else Mexican.

With Warren away for the rest of the afternoon, Gena was free to curl up on the sofa and get herself educated about her dog. Wiley spent the afternoon exploring his new home. From room to room, into every corner, getting to know the spot in the kitchen where Gena had set up one bowl of kibble and another of fresh water, playing with his new toys and shaking the snake, snapping it whip-like in an effort, apparently, to break its neck. Fortunately, the snake was resilient. It became the object of a game in which Gena tossed it off to a distant spot across the living room floor and said, "Get the snake, Wiley! Get the snake," and Wiley, sharp as a tack, was soon bringing it back to her, with an expression that plainly said, like an eager child, "Again, again!"

By four o'clock, they were both worn out. After all, they'd both been through a lot over the last couple of days, and when Warren came home after his day of golf, he found Gena curled up on the sofa, sound asleep, and Wiley curled up against her, also sound asleep.

"God-*damn*!" He was laughing. "You brought that thing home with you." Gena opened up a sleepy eye. So did Wiley. "I thought you were taking him to a shelter. That's what you said before I left this morning."

"I decided to keep him." She sat up, getting herself awake. "I think he's cute."

"Cute? He's weird. Look at him. He's all sharp edges. Nothing cuddly about that animal." Warren went into the kitchen and came back with a bottle of water. "Only you could think he's cute. And what's that hunk of hair on his head? He looks like someone started putting him together and then lost interest." He stared at Wiley for a moment, then laughed. "I bet you gave him a name."

"I did. His name is Wiley."

"He looks like a very tall rat."

"He does not. Stop it, Warren."

"You two are a pair. A pair of beanpoles."

That one really stung. Back in high school, calling her "beanpole" was a good way to make her mad. That, and "giraffe girl." And "whooping crane." And anything else that made fun of her tall, skinny frame.

"That's enough, Warren. I like this dog. I'm keeping him." She was up off the sofa now, collecting Wiley's leash. "I think it's a good time to take a walk. Just Wiley and me. Alone."

"Well, that's fine with me. Any walking of that dog gets done, you're doing it. I don't want to have anything to do with him. I wouldn't even want to be seen with him."

She put the new leash on Wiley.

"Don't worry. You won't have to. He'll be totally my dog. I just hope you're not going to be making fun of him forever."

"Ah, come on, honey. Don't be mad." He came over to her to give her a make-up kiss. "I was just kidding."

But as he got close to Gena, Wiley started to bark. It was a bark that had a message in it, and he bared his teeth and growled a low and menacing growl and Warren backed off awkwardly, banging his leg against the coffee table.

"Oh, now that's just fine," he said, bending to rub the sore spot and looking warily at Wiley, who had his eyes fixed intently on him. Gena started to laugh.

"You think it's funny?" Now Warren was mad. A banged shin really hurts.

"No, of course not." She was still laughing. "I'll have to teach him not to bark at you. But right now, I'm taking him out." She didn't say it, but she liked Wiley's being protective of her. "Maybe you should come along with us after all. You two should be friends."

"No way. That dog is all yours." And as she walked out the door he called after her, "Don't forget: We're having dinner with Dan and Viv. Seven o'clock at Galba's."

Chapter Five

Galba's was a terrific little neighborhood place just around the corner, somewhat dark, comfortably intimate, and a favorite spot for casual, impromptu dinners. Nick Galba watched over his customers like a grandpa, and the wait staff knew to be friendly but not annoying, efficient but not officious. Gena and Warren ate there often. When they arrived that night, Viv and Dan were already at their usual table, a semicircular banquette in the corner. They'd already started on a bottle of a nice Italian red wine and were nibbling at the antipasti.

"You're late," Dan said. He had his phone in his hand. "I was just going to call." He scooted over to make room for Gena to sit next to him.

"We got a little sidetracked," Warren said as he pulled out a chair and sat facing them. "Gena's fault. You tell 'em, Gena." But before Gena could open her mouth, Warren took over. "No, listen, everyone. As of today, without anyone asking me for my opinion, we are now the owners of—wait for it—a *dog!*" Gena made a gesture of irritation, but he went right on. "She found this thing in the woods somewhere, and she brought it home—and it's the ugliest thing you've ever seen. I bet even its mother didn't love it." He turned to Gena with a bright idea that had just occurred to him. "Maybe that's why he was all lost in the woods. Abandoned, poor thing. Even his mother didn't want him."

"Oh, stop it, Warren." To her friends she said, "He's not like that at all. I don't think he's ugly, not a bit. But yes, he is unusual looking. And I like him. I found him when I was driving back from Connecticut. I was up there yesterday on that story I'm doing for *Lady Fair*. I told you, Viv, the one about Romy deVere. It was raining and—"

Warren broke in. "And he's so pathetic. He doesn't have any hair on him except what's on the top of his head—he looks like Woody Woodpecker. So weird looking. A skinny little dog on these skinny long legs, like he's on stilts. I can see why Gena likes him—he's a beanpole like her. Right, honey? Did you recognize a kindred spirit? Two peas in a skinny pod?"

"Warren's mad because the dog doesn't like him. He barked at him, wouldn't let him near me."

Dan chuckled. "Sounds like the dog has good taste."

"Very funny. I thought he wanted to rip my throat out."

"Oh, it wasn't so bad," Gena said. "I thought it was kind of sweet, him being so protective of me."

"Yeah. Well, he better learn to behave or you're going to have to get rid of him."

There was beginning to be an unfriendly tension at the table, so Viv deflected the conversation.

"I bet I recognize the breed," she said. "He sounds like a Chinese Crested. Skinny? Long legs? Hairless except for, like, on its head and paws?"

"Oh, Viv. You're so smart." Gena was impressed. "Yes, that's what the vet told me. And I've been doing some research." Gena took a breadstick from the basket and nibbled on it. "How do you know about Cresteds? The vet told me they're kind of rare."

"Rare is right," Warren muttered. "He looks like a Dr. Seuss animal."

Viv ignored Warren's snarking. "We did a design job for this couple on Park Avenue. Fabulous apartment, lots of money, twelve rooms. They were redoing their entryway. The van Siclens. Harriet and Russ van Siclen. Nice people, and they had this little dog that had masses of hair, like a sunburst of white silk, and only her sharp nose and these two pointy ears sticking out. Mrs. van S said it was a Powderpuff. She said there was also a hairless version, and she showed me pictures. That's what your dog seems to be."

"I remember now," Warren said. "I knew that dog reminded me of something. He reminds me of Sneetches. Remember Sneetches? From Dr. Seuss? Yellow, with a couple of hairs sticking up all wiry on his head? That's what this dog looks like."

"Oh, he does not! Honestly, Warren!" Gena dug her phone out of her bag. "I've got pictures of him," Gena said. She already had a Wiley album set up on her phone, and she was scrolling through to find the pics. "His name is Wiley. You know, like Wile E. Coyote."

"Oh, I can't believe this." Warren's irritation was unmistakable. "Now you're going to start showing pictures. You'd think you'd given birth to him. For God's sake, can we stop talking about this damn dog?"

He signaled the waiter to come over.

"Warren, why don't you let Gena have a little fun with this," Dan said. "It's a big deal, adding a pet to a family."

But Warren had his own agenda, and it wasn't about dogs. "Gena, put that phone away. With all the attention on that rat-dog, I can't get a word in." He sat back in his chair, looking suddenly expansive. When all eyes were on him, he said, "Listen, everyone. I've got some *real* news." He looked briefly at the menu and told the waiter to bring him a steak—rare—a salad, and a vodka martini. "But go ahead and order. I'll wait till you're done."

And he did wait, which gave him time to savor his news while Gena ordered pasta. Viv ordered shrimp and said she'd also have some of Dan's pizza. Nick Galba's pizzas were famous, thin crust, and irresistible—Dan always ordered one. Except for Warren, they stayed with the red wine. The waiter collected their menus and left.

"Okay," Dan said. "Now you have the floor. Go ahead, Warren. What's the news?"

"I tried to tell Gena when I got home this afternoon, but that dog was there and there was a whole kerfuffle about him, so I got sidetracked." Warren paused, keeping his big news to himself for another few moments. Then, when he was sure they were all listening, he announced, "So the boss asked me to come along for some golf this morning. At his club. Marlin Weggeland himself."

Dan's face registered his respect for this impressive news. Gena forgot about her annoyance with Warren; this *was* important news. Viv just said, "Go on," slowly, definitely attentive.

"Well, all through our game we just talked about the course, and about the weather. And the latest from Washington, and the New York politics, the mayoral race, the latest scandal. You know—just small talk, casual. But I could feel that he was checking me out, seeing how I handled myself." Warren's smile was a little sly and a lot self-satisfied. "He's a pretty good golfer, but I'm better, so it took a little doing for me to let him beat me, which I did, of course, but not by much, because I want him to respect me. The whole time, there was not one word about work or the office until we finished our game. And it was only later, when we were in the clubhouse having a drink together"—again, Warren paused, savoring the moment—"when Marlin Weggeland told me that management has been watching my work on the Isler project and they were impressed that, young as I am, I'm really on top of things and..." Warren paused again, took a deep breath, and said, "They're putting me in charge of the whole team!"

"Oh, Warren." Beyond those two words, Gena was speechless. She knew how much this vote of confidence meant to Warren, and she was truly delighted for him.

"It might even mean a new title," Warren added.

"Jesus, that's great. Congratulations, Warren." Dan lifted his glass. "Here's to New York's next billionaire. We wish you lots of luck." The others joined in, lifting their glasses and drinking to him.

Wordlessly, Gena let her eyes meet his and signaled *I'm so glad for you.* And Warren's smile let her know he got her message. He was basking in this moment.

The rest of the dinner was devoted to Warren, his current success, and his future in the world of investment banking. And Gena was okay with letting him have the limelight. There'd been too much talk about her, and she knew Warren was happier when all eyes were on him.

She said no more about the dog. And she didn't mention anything more about the interview with Romy deVere in Connecticut. That could wait. And anyway, she needed more time to think about Romy.

But all through dinner, she realized something every dog owner knows: If you own a dog, you are no longer a totally free person. In a restaurant, at the theater, in church, wherever you may be, you know there's someone at home, someone who not only misses you, but also needs you.

Wiley needed to be walked!

And so Gena realized, as they were all examining the dessert menu and making their choices, that she couldn't just hang out at Galba's for as long as she might like, for as long as they usually did, for as long as it suited Warren to go on talking about his wonderful new opportunities. While the two men ordered chocolate cake with ice cream—as they always did—and Viv agonized over the diet-friendly bowl of fresh berries or her favorite, the spumoni, Gena was looking at her watch and thinking, *I don't even know if Wiley's housebroken. I hope he's all right. I hope he can wait till I get back. Should I just leave without Warren? Not a good idea—he's already not happy about my having Wiley.*

She decided to say nothing; she'd stay to have coffee and dessert, and then as soon and as tactfully as possible, plead fatigue or a headache and get Warren to leave.

She opened the menu and scanned the desserts. Poor Gena, she was afflicted with a metabolism that burned up calories faster than she could consume them. As hard as she pushed the carbs, as much as she ate ice cream by the carton, as dutifully as she chose the richest desserts, and every night (ever since childhood) drank a bedtime glass of warm milk with a couple of Oreo cookies, she remained reed-slim. While other women suffered with their extra pounds and the ups and downs of diet successes and failures, spending fortunes on spas and gyms and yoga classes and Pilates sessions, trying, *trying so hard!* to slim themselves down, Gena longed for voluptuous curves. Or at least a small amount of body fat she could pinch between her thumb and forefinger. And she did not believe, not even for a minute, that the many women who told her they envied her slim figure really meant it. How could they? How could anyone envy a girl who felt like a beanpole, like a gangly whooping crane, like a giraffe girl, like a stick figure walking around on stilts—all the teasing names she'd heard since childhood—a girl who tried so hard, with pleated skirts and horizontal stripes and big, bulky coats, to make herself look less awkward, less stringy, less sharp-edged.

Viv, her friend since sixth grade, always understood. She didn't torment her by doing the usual reassuring and cheering-up that most women offered when she vented about her looks. Viv knew that it was a rare woman who liked what she saw in the mirror, and if her friend really felt like a lanky scarecrow, the magical formula had not yet been invented that would convince her that she was just fine. The best she could say about any woman's preoccupation with her weight was: "It's like the stock market. It goes up. It goes down. And nobody knows why."

So Gena studied the menu and ordered the tiramisu with extra crème fraîche, and when the desserts arrived at the table, she was willing also to take a taste of Viv's spumoni and Warren's chocolate cake.

Warren had had another martini, so he was feeling really good as they walked back to their place. Alfie was on, and Warren gave him a big hello. There was no one in the elevator and as soon as the door closed, he got Gena into his arms, ignoring the not-so-concealed security camera up in the corner that Gena was pointing to. "So what," he said. "Let him look. Can't a guy kiss his girl when he's got something really big to celebrate? When the whole world is his oyster and he's feeling ready to take it on?"

He was still kissing her when the elevator door opened at the forty-first floor.

And still as he fumbled for his key, got it into the lock, and got the door open.

And would still have been kissing her as they got into the apartment if it weren't for the barking and carrying-on that started up around their feet.

"God-*damn!*"

Warren was not a man to kick a dog, but if ever in his life he came close, this was the moment.

"I'll take him out," Gena said quickly. She scooped Wiley up off the floor and into her arms. She whispered into Wiley's ear, "*Shh. Shh*, Wiley," as she put on his leash. "You and Warren are going to have to get along, or you won't be able to stay."

Wiley was quiet in her arms, but over her shoulder he and Warren glared at each other, and each one's expression was clear: *I've got my eye on you!*

And later that night, Warren made it clear that Wiley was not welcome in the bedroom. "That dog is not coming in here with us," he announced. And under his breath, as he shut Wiley out, he muttered, "So now I'm supposed to close the door to my own bedroom, in my own home?"

Chapter Six

Another beautiful day. Gena didn't want to wake Warren so she got out of bed quietly, dressed quietly, and quietly got Wiley's leash on him. They made it into the elevator without making a sound. Out on the street, New York was in its early Sunday morning gentleness, its streets silent and empty and all the shops not yet open. In the park, the morning sun, just coming up over the East River, lighted up the tops of the trees, turning them all golden.

Early morning runners were out and a few bicycle riders, along with other dog owners, who gave brief nods to each other, all moving at that easy, contemplative, Sunday morning pace that accommodates a dog's interest in sniffing his or her way along their path, when there's no rush to get to the office and the only thing waiting at home is bagels and cream cheese and the *New York Times*.

Gena took her time getting back to the apartment, where she found a note from Warren:

> *Had a call from the office. Something's come up. And I'm going to play tennis. Don't be lonely. (You and that mutt can spend the day together.) Home by dinner.*
> ☺

She wasn't sorry. Her head was buzzing with ideas, and a few quiet hours would be a good thing. She put fresh water into Wiley's bowl and added a cup of kibble to the crumbs that were left from yesterday. Then she brewed up some coffee, scrambled a couple of eggs, added two sausage links and some toast with lots of butter, and put a doughnut she'd picked up at the corner bakery onto a separate plate. At the breakfast island in the kitchen, she laid out her plates and put a yellow legal pad and a pen next to them. And as she ate, she worked on her agenda for Monday:

1. Call Viv. Meet with Harriet van Siclen? Contact info?
(Learn more about this breed)
2. Pitch something to Marge about a New York dogs story.
Rich dogs/poor dogs? Lifestyles
Westminster Kennel Club—dog show. (When?)
Dog fashion, accessories, costs (range? fancy—plain)
Costs, generally.
Laws?
Homeless?
Compare—city dogs, suburban, country?
Do city dogs suffer, confined to apartments? (Really?)

She looked at Wiley, who was curled up on the pillow she'd put in the corner for him.

"Are you suffering?" she asked him. Wiley opened an eye, acknowledged her question, dismissed it, and went back to sleep.

When she was a kid, her dad wouldn't let her have a dog. Besides being allergic, he insisted it was wrong to keep a dog shut up in a confined space, allowed out only for walks, and only on the owner's schedule. And her mom was sure every dog was out to get her. So there was no question about it—there would be no pets in her home. Until this morning, she'd never even thought about it. But now?

Now there really was no question about it.

She looked at her funny little dog, with his random tufts of hair, his long, long legs, and his utterly improbably skinny little self, and she realized the truth:

She'd fallen in love. She and Wiley were kindred spirits. Fate—or something—had brought them together.

Warren could object all he wanted. He and Wiley would have to learn to get along, because this was her dog and she was now totally committed to him.

And then she turned to item number three on her list:

3. Romy deVere
There's something there????
Need to get into the archives. First thing on Monday!!!

Chapter Seven

She absolutely *loved* working at *Lady Fair*. Each time she entered the building, she felt the same magic when the elevator doors opened up onto the thirty-sixth floor. Everything about the *Lady Fair* offices delighted her, the spare, sleek design of the work spaces, incongruously almost obliterated by the jumbled, overflowing excess of stuff, stuff, and more stuff, from the masses of shoes collected on shelves to the randomly parked racks of dresses and pants and jeans and skirts, the photos tacked up everywhere, thick as wallpaper, the accessories—the belts and gloves and hats—stuffed into fashion niches and crammed into cubbyholes, the curling irons and electric razors pushed under desks and tossed into file cabinets with stacks of papers, articles, works-in-progress, notes, and memos, all piled up precariously on desktops and file cabinets with photos of family members nestled and tilted and jammed up against potted plants and cups full of pencils. Cosmetics flowed in a steady stream from companies eager to get their newest product into *Lady Fair*. Thick and fast the stuff came, every day, creams and lotions and gels and foams and oils in bright colors and brilliant packaging. Seductive tubes of lipstick and pots of blush and little tubs of concealers and foundations. New perfumes and hair products, enough to dazzle whole villages of beauty-eager women of all ages, from dreamy little girls to hopeful eighty-year-olds, tumbling-over stacks of boxes and elegantly designed and beribboned bags of beauty products perched on every surface, on the "guest" chair, on top of cabinets, on bracketed shelves.

Four years now, and Gena had not lost the excitement she'd felt from day one, when they took her on only a year out of college, first as an intern and then as a features writer, assistant to the features editor, Dinah Featherington.

This morning, as she arrived with a Starbucks latte in hand and her big tote bag swinging from her shoulder, she stopped to poke her head in at Annelie Magano's office. "Nell, honey," she said. (Annelie was the beauty editor's given name, but she'd become Nell when she'd entered a first-grade classroom graced with six girls who had Ann-like names.) "Do you have a lipstick or a gloss or something? I was so late this morning, there was no time—"

"Come on in," Nell said. She was used to being the go-to person for all cosmetic needs around the office. This was a precious perk of a beauty editor's job. The massive quantity of free product was hers to use as she pleased—which was mainly to keep her co-workers looking lovely, and to hand out lavishly as gifts to friends and family. Now she did a quick scan of Gena's outfit, starting at her feet: beige ballet flats, burnt-orange blouson dress, broad brown belt riding low on the hip, all covered with a cropped, cream-colored jacket. Then Nell swiveled her chair around to face the clutter on her desk. There was always something amid the jumble that would be just the thing. She poked through the unruly pile of cosmetics, a pile she kept pushed back just far enough to clear some space for her to work, and fished through the mass of creams and shampoos and body scrubs and bath gels until, as always, she found the right item.

"This should work," she said, holding up a sleek black tube. "A new color from Lancôme. Very subtle, should work perfectly."

"Thanks a bunch," Gena said. "This'll get me through the day." And she rushed off to her office.

She kept the reason she was running late this morning to herself.

Actually, it wasn't her fault. If Warren hadn't turned off the alarm, she'd have been up at seven and out by eight. Plenty of time to get properly ready for the day. But the clock said 8:10 when she opened her eyes, and it was the Bloomberg business news blaring from the kitchen that woke her. Warren had already shaved, dressed, and was brewing the coffee when she opened her eyes. He'd have let her sleep all morning.

"Oh, God!" She sent the duvet flying and ran barefoot to the bathroom. "I won't even have time to shower. Warren!" she shouted down the hall at him. "How *could* you?"

"Take it easy, hon," he called back from the kitchen. "What's the big deal? It's not like it's the end of the world if you sleep in one morning."

She brushed her teeth at top speed and didn't bother to answer him. She knew what Warren thought of her job, like it didn't matter if she was late for work. "Fluff stuff for airheads," he'd called it when she first started working at *Lady Fair*. "Gena's doing her bit for the world of lotions and potions," he'd say to friends. Like he thought it was on a par with babysitting. Or being a school monitor. It was an old issue between them, but it was not the time for an argument, not the time for Warren's notions. She made a face at herself in the mirror and decided there was no time for makeup.

"And I need to walk Wiley! Oh, God!"

She needed to be moving, and fast. With a twist of her long, bright hair into a scraggly bun, with a stick pick to hold it together, she got herself quickly dressed, grabbed her handbag off the doorknob where she always hung it, and snatched her jacket from the chair where she'd last dropped it.

"Honestly, Warren."

"I thought you'd like a few extra Z's."

"You just don't get it," she said as she attached the leash to Wiley's collar. And she was out the door.

* * * *

She put her Starbucks cup on her desk, pulled her notebooks and her to do list out of the tote bag, and laid them next to the coffee. She slipped out of her jacket and draped it over the back of her chair. She was just opening up her computer when the phone on her desk rang.

"You there?" It was Viv calling.

"Viv. I was just going to call you."

"Why? What's up?"

"The other night, you mentioned a client of yours, Harriet van Siclen. You said she had a Powderpuff Crested. I'm working on a story idea, and she might be a good person to talk to."

"What's the story?"

"I'm thinking of doing something about New York dogs. How being a dog in New York affects a dog's life. Just kicking it around at this point. You know, clothes, accessories, high-rise apartment living. No backyards. Rich dogs, poor dogs. Like their owners. Lots of angles."

"Sounds like a great idea. I can give her a call and let you know if it's okay with her. I'll text you her contact information."

"You're a peach, Viv."

"No problem. But I want to hear about your trip to Connecticut. Your interview with Romy deVere? You never got to tell us at dinner."

"I wanted to, but Warren was so full of his great news, I just let it go. Maybe we can have lunch or something—"

But just then the intern, Selma, stuck her head around the corner, signaling for Gena's attention. Gena held up a finger to tell Selma to hold on a minute.

"Listen, Viv, I'm kind of backed up here right now. Maybe later in the week. We can talk about it then. Lots to tell you."

"Okay. Give me a call."

"Okay. Bye now." She hung up and motioned Selma to come in.

"Morning, Selma. You need me?"

"Ira Garlen wants to talk to you about the deVere shoot. Soon as you get in, he said. They're setting up the schedule now."

"Right. Thanks, Selma. And we'll need Nell and her people in on this, too. I'll let her know, okay?"

* * * *

An hour later, when she got back from her meeting with Ira and his staff, there was a voicemail from Viv:

"Gena, I called Harriet but we were interrupted. I didn't get a chance to explain why you wanted to talk to her. I could hear someone talking to her and it sounded sort of urgent. She just said, 'Yes, yes, have her call me. I must go now. Sorry.' And she hung up. So I guess you can go ahead and contact her. I'm texting her phone number and address to you now. And her dog's name is Sweetie Pie. But she's mostly called the Pie. Or just Pie."

Before she called Harriet van Siclen, she went first to Wikipedia's images. The photos showed a woman, mid-fortyish, rail-thin, and very elegant, with a perfect upswept coif, a skillful blond color job, perfect skin, careful makeup, a Chanel outfit, and serious jewelry. And among beautiful settings—gala balls, Paris streets, upscale restaurants, and one where Gena hoped to meet her: at home, on a pale sofa, big windows behind her, and lush draperies. On her lap, cozy and comfortable, was a small dog full of thick fluff, with long ears, a pointy snout, and an alert expression. Woman and dog, both looking directly into the camera with intelligent, engaging eyes. The woman looked very calm. The dog looked ready to play.

It wasn't Harriet van Siclen who answered the phone, "The van Siclen residence."

"Hello. This is Gena Shaw from *Lady Fair*. May I speak to Mrs. van Siclen?"

"Just a moment, please."

There was a wait of a minute.

A new voice

"Hello. Is this Gena? Vivian Dorrance said you'd be calling me."

Before Gena could say hello, Mrs. van Siclen broke in on her. "The thing is, dear, it's absolutely the worst time. I'd just *love* to talk to you, I really would. I'm so completely fond of *Lady Fair,* I read it *religiously,* never miss an issue. But the thing is, I'm in the midst of *packing,* of all things. Practically out of the blue, with practically no word of warning, Russell—Russell is my husband—is being transferred—to *Australia* of all places, can you imagine—and I've just got thousands of things to do. So I really don't see how I could possibly—"

At this point, Gena broke in.

"Oh, that really is such a shame," she said. "Vivian said she knew the timing was difficult, but she thought you'd certainly love to see a story about Sweetie Pie in *Lady Fair,* and you might be able to find a bit of time, if I managed to be very, *very* efficient and not get in the way of your arrangements."

There was a silence for a very long minute.

"You'd write about my Sweetie Pie?"

"Oh, yes." Gena sensed a propitious shift in the momentum here. "We'd definitely be focusing the piece on Sweetie Pie."

Another long pause.

"With pictures?"

"Of course." After a couple of silent beats, she added, "Possibly we'd want to feature her on the cover—"

She heard a sigh.

She waited.

"I suppose just a quick break in the day wouldn't be a problem. If it could really be quite quick—"

"Oh, yes. Of course. I'd make it quite quick. What time is good?"

"This afternoon—maybe at three?"

"Three o'clock would be perfect. And the address, Mrs. van Siclen?"

"Call me Harriet, dear."

"You're very kind, Harriet."

"We're at six twelve Park Avenue."

"I'll be there at three."

Chapter Eight

Gena looked at her watch. Was there time enough to run down the couple of floors to *Lady Fair*'s cafeteria, grab a sandwich, and get back to her desk? She'd need a couple of hours to pay proper attention to Romy deVere and the story she felt sure was lurking somewhere in the innocent stack of notes she'd come away with. She decided she was too eager to get started. She could get some lunch later; she'd pick up something before she met with Mrs. van Siclen.

Anyway, she'd have to stop off at her apartment first, because Wiley needed to be walked—and she was going to have to figure out what to do about *that*. She couldn't go running home every day in the middle of her busy work schedule.

It must be a little like having a child at home. Well, not quite *the same thing, of course—*

On a Post-it, she wrote: Dog walkers? Seferino, maybe? She stuck the note on the edge of her computer.

Then she got out her folder of notes from that meeting with Romy. She opened a new folder in the computer file and begin to write:

> *Romy deVere*
> *Hollywood star, once considered "the most beautiful woman in the world"*
> *97 years old*
> *Healthy, independent*
> *Living in seclusion on a wooded estate in Connecticut (a maid, Martha Baxley, not live-in, comes in every day)*
> *Brilliant career in Hollywood*

Now retired, with her big Newfoundland puppy (some
puppy—nearly knocked me over. Dog's name is Qualtinger, but
she calls him Karl)
   Last ten years, brand new career: painting
   Does fabulous work—has been showing in local galleries
   In her youth—exquisite, dark-haired, sultry, intriguing
   Perfect features, perfect figure
   And still very beautiful
   Did some scandalous, racy early movies
   Famously a "free" spirit
   Much married—six husbands, two children (bio details in the
file)
   Born in Vienna, Austria, May 14, 1919—at the end of the
First World War
   Was 19 years old in 1938—already a working actress (at the
Reinhardt Theatre in Vienna.)
   1938: Austria in turmoil—the annexation by Germany
   Family escaped, got themselves to America

Gena stopped writing. She focused on that interview. There was a
moment there, as she and Romy talked, when she'd felt a kind of a subtext
running under Romy's comments—like when a second theme plays, barely
audible, under the main song. A kind of harmony.

Or maybe it was more of a discord.

There was something she said. What was it? What was it she said?
What could it be? I'd asked her about her name...I'd asked if she was of
French descent...

Gena turned on her recorder and played back that portion of the tape:

   "Oh, my dear, the name is ridiculous."

There was that lovely voice, with its velvet undertones, lightly accented.

   "I arrived in Hollywood with an entirely different name.
I was Lotte Elisabeth Kanfer, but it was thought to be too
German—the US was then on the brink of war with Germany,
so they made up a new name for me. It mattered not at all to
me. I wanted only to be out of Austria and safe in America, and
I was eager to work. I was, after all, only nineteen years old.
What does one know at that age?"

"My father—ah, my papa...Thomas Kanfer. Tommy,
everyone called him. He was an engineer, you know. Quite
brilliant. And so advanced for his time. He thought women
were entitled to full lives independent of any man's wishes. He
encouraged me to work and to be educated, and to let no man
arrange my life for me, let no man be my master. He shared so
much of his work and his thinking with me. So much, indeed,
I could almost, if I wished, make my living as an electrical
engineer."

I remember now. She looked at me as though she wanted to share a
secret. What kind of secret could she possibly have? She's been in the
public eye, scrutinized intimately by thousands of people, had thousands
of articles written about her, thousands of interviews—what can there be
about her that has not been revealed, explored, exposed to a fare-thee-
well. All those husbands, six of them, and her children. And a few scandals
along the way. And if she did have some sort of secret, why would she be
trying to share it with me? Without coming right out and saying what it
is? I must be imagining—

But still, there was *something*. Gena's good journalistic instincts were
at work, and she'd long ago learned to pay attention to the messages her
instincts sent her.

She replayed that last bit of tape. Romy had looked intently into her
eyes as she'd said those last words.

"...he shared so much of his work and his thinking with me.
So much, indeed, I could almost, if I wished, make my living as
an electrical engineer."

"Hmm. There's something there...something there..."

Time to shift gears. Time for Gena to change the writer's hat to the
researcher's. Time to go to Google.

Start at the root. Go back to Tommy Kanfer, the father. And the
husbands—all six of them!

An hour later, Gena was staring at a sheaf of printouts, stunned by
what she had uncovered.

The first item, on top of the pile of papers, was an application to the
United States Patent Office, dated June 1941, made by Thomas Kanfer
and Liesl Hardtmann.

Their application describes their invention as a "radio steering device... secret communication systems using carrier waves of different frequencies... for the remote control of torpedoes and aerial craft...simple and reliable in operation...difficult to discover or decipher...an enemy would be unable to determine at what frequency a controlling impulse would be sent..." Attached were schematics and diagrams.

Below that first set of papers was a stack of scholarly articles, and current articles written within the last couple of years, that traced the advanced electronic technology of our time, the "frequency-hopping spread spectrum" of Wi-Fi and Bluetooth, of GPS and CDMI, back to their beginning in Kanfer and Hardtmann's 1941 wartime radio guidance system. (Google explained that CDMI stands for "Cloud Data Management Interface.")

Actually, her Google sleuthing had been easier than she'd expected. Starting with Thomas Kanfer—that had been a simple start. He was Romy's father. And Hardtmann? That took a moment longer, till something in her memory bank clicked and connected to a name in the list of Romy's husbands. Sure enough, there it was: Just a quick look at the file on Romy and she read that Romy's first husband, the much older man she'd married when she was barely 17, was Hans Hardtmann! And she had still been married to him when she and her father escaped from Austria, before she went on to become a fabulous Hollywood star—one of the all-time greats. And then it was only a couple of mental associations that led her from Liesl Hardtmann to Lotte Elisabeth—or to Elisabeth's diminutive form, *Liesl*! So it was as Liesl Hardtmann that Romy filed, with her father, the application for the patent they'd invented together!

How could Gena *not* be stunned?

Not only had the stunningly beautiful Romy deVere, together with her father, helped the Allies win the war, but their creation reached down decades, to the present day; they were actually among the founders of the electronic world we're living in today.

My God! That's incredible. That's absolutely incredible!

Gena sat back in her chair. She needed to take some deep breaths. Maybe ten or twenty.

Romy deVere, world-famous, international beauty and glamorous, successful Hollywood star, had a secret life as Lotte Elizabeth (Liesl) Kanfer Hardtmann, engineer, inventor, and the brains behind a profoundly innovative technological breakthrough, a breakthrough that was not only of major military significance, but also effectively civilization-changing.

So why did she keep it a secret? I'm surprised it wasn't publicized extensively...

I'm sure she wanted me to know. So why couldn't she just tell me directly? Why be so secretive about it? Why be so mysterious?

Gena looked at her watch.

Well, whatever the reason, I've got to get going now. Need to check in on Wiley. And I have that appointment with Mrs. van Siclen at three.

But all the way uptown, even as she took Wiley for a quick walk around the block, and then in the cab on the way to six twelve Park Avenue, her mind was on Romy and the amazing secret of her wartime past. It was certainly something she'd explore with her at the photo shoot next week.

But in the meantime, am I supposed to keep her secret? Surely Romy is experienced enough to know, if you want to keep a secret, you don't tell it to a journalist. No, if you tell a secret to a journalist, you mean to expose the secret. So why now? After all these years. And why in this oblique way, without really telling me anything, practically expecting me to read her mind? And am I ready to share it with Marge? I have an obligation to tell my editor in chief, don't I? And Dinah? And what about Viv? I always tell her everything. And Warren, too. I never keep secrets from him. But this isn't my secret, so nothing to Viv and nothing to Warren.

For the time being, she was going to say nothing to anyone. It could wait until she had more information, if Romy was willing to add to what she'd already learned.

Chapter Nine

The maid opened the door. Behind her, brilliant sunlight flooded a long hallway and a distant drawing room beyond, in which the drapes had been drawn back and great glass doors had been opened to the soft afternoon breeze. A terrace was visible beyond them.

"Mrs. van Siclen is expecting you." She gave Gena a small and proper smile. Her uniform was gray, with a starched white half-apron and white collar and cuffs. She turned, and Gena followed her through the hallway.

The drawing room was done in gentle colors, cream and beige. Paintings on the walls, soft sofas and chairs grouped around a coffee table. A Cartier perfume—La Panthère—hovered over everything, along with the scent of good leather and polished wood. The room would have been a perfection of serenity and ease, except—

Except that today it was a mess of boxes, piles of clothes here and there, wads of tissue paper strewn about.

And deep in the sofa, surrounded by billowy pillows, was Mrs. Russell van Siclen, *née* Harriet Adele Brackman. On any other day, Harriet would have been a vision of calm and composed elegance, expensive haute couture, perfect coif, some impressive gold accessories and a well-toned, well-massaged, suitably buff figure. But on this day, Harriet was frantic, surrounded by more tissue paper, lists of things to do, marking pens, and stuff, lots of *stuff*! A strand of hair had come astray from her perfect upswept hairdo. She waved Gena toward an armchair at her right.

"Come in, dear. Come in." Harriet put the pen and notepaper onto the coffee table in front of her. She brushed at the loose strand of hair, trying unsuccessfully to tuck it back in place, and seemed to be saying, *it's all just too much!*

Gena was about to sit down, but the chair was already filled with something silky and long-haired. She caught herself just as two big brown eyes and a pointy snout turned up toward her.

"Oh, don't mind the Pie," Harriet said. "She's perfectly friendly. Just push her away." As Gena hesitated, Harriet said, "Over here, Pie." She patted the cushion next to her. "Come sit here with me." The Pie seemed to have a perfect understanding of the English language—with a jump down and another jump up, she was nestling in beside Mrs. van Siclen. "And don't worry. She hardly sheds at all, and she was brushed this morning." She paused, reflectively. "She's absolutely the best dog in the whole world. I'm going to miss her so much."

As Gena sat down, Harriet said, "It's just all so sudden. I had no warning at all. The bank is transferring Russell to Australia." She didn't stop to explain that Russell was her husband, as though of course Gena would know. "He'll be in charge of setting up a new operation in Melbourne, and we're leaving day after tomorrow. The men are coming to pack us up, and I have to decide what stays and what goes. Heaven knows when we'll be back. It's exciting, of course, and a marvelous opportunity for Russell, but the awful thing is, the Pie can't come with us." Gena had no chance to offer the appropriate word of sympathy or ask a question. "Australia has these dreadful laws about dogs coming into the country. A hundred and eighty days of quarantine. Just think. I wouldn't dream of putting Sweetie Pie through that. And I have no idea how long we're going to be there. Russell says it could be a couple of years. Poor Pie. But she'll be with Paul, so she'll be all right. Won't you, Sweetie, you poor thing?" She put a kiss on the top of the dog's head, who responded with a little lick at her nose. "That's Paul over there," Mrs. van Siclen said. "On the phone, as usual."

With a gesture, she pointed to the study, just through the arch into the next room, where Gena saw a tall man in a dark gray business suit talking intently into his cell phone. He was standing near a floor-to-ceiling window, silhouetted against the bright sunlight. His back was turned to them.

"Paul," Harriet called to him. "This is Gena Shaw, from *Lady Fair.* She's doing a story on Cresteds."

Paul turned and nodded briefly in Gena's direction. His attention was on his telephone conversation.

"Don't mind him," Harriet said. "He's always on his phone. You just get comfy and I'll have Mimi get you a cup of coffee. Or would you prefer tea?"

"Coffee would be lovely. Thank you."

Without a word between them or any signal that Gena could see, Mimi, who had been waiting discreetly in the doorway, turned and left the room.

Harriet called again to the man in the next room. "Paul, please get off the phone and give me a hand here."

Paul slipped the phone into his pocket. "Sorry, sis," he said. "They need me at the office. This minute. Gotta go." As he passed through the room, he said, "Don't worry. I'll pick up the Pie in the morning and say goodbye then." And with a nod to Gena, he added, "Nice to have met you."

And he was gone. Gena knew he never caught her name.

She opened her bag and got out her notepad and pencil, ready to begin the interview. "I know you're busy today, and I really appreciate your taking the time to talk to me. I'll keep it as quick as possible."

"I see you use paper and pencil. So old-fashioned. That's nice. And pencil, not pen."

Gena smiled. You have lovely things here. This fabric"—she touched the cushion next to her—"is an imported Italian silk, isn't it? A pen could do damage here."

"You have a good eye," Harriet said.

Mimi rolled in a little glass-and-brass cart. Harriet served coffee with some fragile, lightly spiced sugar cookies. While they talked, Sweetie Pie dozed in the comfort of Harriet's lap and attended, occasionally, to the women's conversation. And for an hour or so, while the shadows gradually lengthened across the city, Harriet talked to Gena about the pleasures—and problems—of owning a Chinese Crested.

"And my dear, there are fabulous Crested Facebook friends all over the world. You can't imagine the hundreds, maybe thousands of people—I see their posts from Indonesia and Lithuania and Peru, and of course here in the states, from everywhere imaginable—people who share their fun, their difficulties, their experiences. Help each other out, send photos, little videos. Help find homes for rescue dogs. Design and make fabulous doggie coats and dog beds and dog booties. They share medical tips about their pets, and warnings about medical problems. And they really get to be friends. Like conventional friends, they talk about their lives beyond their dogs—their work, their families, poems they've written and pictures they've painted, and recipes they've tried, or even invented."

"I hadn't realized. So there's a whole world out there—"

"Yes, just Google—oh, for example 'naked dog enthusiast club,' and it will steer you in the right direction. There are Crested clubs you can sign on to. You can learn about medical care and the special foods these dogs need, and things to watch out for. The hairless ones, of course, oh, you have to be so careful because their exposed skin makes them so vulnerable. Special soaps, special sunscreens, special oils. You *must* get a supply of coconut oil."

Harriet was now well into her favorite subject, and she forgot all about her packing. Gena was taking page after page of notes. And then a clock chimed in another room and Gena glanced at her watch.

"Oh, I hadn't meant to keep you so long. I promised to be quick. And I do need to get back to my office. I want to begin working on this piece right away. But we will want to contact you about photos. And," she added, smiling, "now that I'm a dog owner, I need to remember that dogs need to be walked."

And then there were the leave-takings, and the well wishes—for Gena, good luck with her article, and for Harriet, best wishes for her transfer to Australia.

And Gena left.

Chapter Ten

"Well, you're looking like the cat that swallowed the canary." Warren eyed Gena up and down.

"I do?"

"You sure do. What's up?" He laid the paper he'd been studying down onto a stack of folders on the sofa next to him.

"Nothing's up. You're imagining things."

Wiley had started barking the minute Gena opened the door, and he was dancing excitedly around her feet as she came into the living room. She put her things down on the coffee table, next to Wiley's leash. As she knelt on the floor to get him ready to go out, she looked up at Warren and gave him a long look.

"Looks to me like you're the one who's been eating a canary," she said. "Do you have some news?"

"Funny you should ask." Warren was beaming. "It just so happens I do have some news." He stood up and preened a little bit. Puffed out his chest. "I told you I wasn't going to be a lowly analyst forever." He opened his arms wide, inviting her to come and congratulate him. "Meet the bank's newest associate. Just got the news this afternoon."

"Oh, Warren. That is so great!" She stood up, about to give him an enthusiastic hug, but as she got close to him, there was Wiley, getting in the way, barking fiercely. "Stop it, Wiley," she said sharply. "Stop barking!" Little good it did. Wiley was determined.

"Can't you shut that dog up? I swear, Gena, if this is how it's going to be, that dog is going to have to go."

"I'm sorry, Warren. I really am. I'll have to figure out how to teach him to be quiet. I'll take him out now, so he won't bother you." She picked Wiley up, shushing him. "Maybe you could order in some dinner while I'm out."

"I already did. I felt like celebrating, so I called for some Indian food."

She didn't say anything. Warren loved Indian food. She didn't. She knew he knew she didn't love Indian food. But he was entitled to a celebration, she thought, so she decided to let it go.

"I won't be long," she said. "And you can tell me all about it when I get back."

"Yeah. Well, don't be long. The food will be here any minute."

She was still carrying Wiley when she got to the elevator, and only then did it occur to her to put him down. She was feeling a little rattled. She didn't like it when Warren was irritated—it always made her feel she'd done something wrong—and now Warren was pissed, she could tell. He was in the middle of his big news and here she was being attentive to Wiley when Warren expected all the attention to be on him. And on top of that, he was probably hungry and wanted to start right in on dinner, and now he'd have to wait for her—and for Wiley—to get back.

And he was right about how she looked: all full of secrets. She was bursting to tell him about the day she'd had—and what a day it had been! Such a rich feast of new experiences—deVere's dramatic hidden history, so full of fascinating twists. And the meeting with the elegant Harriet van Siclen and her beautiful Pie. But it would have to wait. Warren wouldn't want to hear about anything about dogs, that was for sure. And as for Romy's adventures back in the war—well the tabloids would love it, but this was *Lady Fair*'s story. She wanted to do this right. She'd talk to Marge about it in the morning. And she'd wait for more from Romy.

As for Warren—no, she'd wait with that. After all, Gena was no gossip, and this was Romy's secret. She should wait till they'd had a chance to talk.

When she and Wiley got off the elevator, the whole forty-first floor was redolent with the aromas of the East. Warren was already transferring everything into bowls, the saffron rice and the platters of naan, the mounds of *malai kofta*. This was his favorite kind of evening. Ensconced on the living room sofa, the bowls of beef *tikka masala* and a plate of samosas spread across the coffee table and a movie on the TV. With Gena curled up next to him. And then, later, in the dark, with only the ambient light from the city around them that seemed to float in through the tall glass windows, making love in their big bed, their "play pen," he liked to call it. And then a sound sleep, and up the next morning to go out and be a master of the universe again. Warren Haglund was on his way up, and all was right with the world. Except—

Except that now, before Gena could come to bed, she had to take Wiley out for his last walk of the night. And Warren had to wait. Which kind of spoiled the evening's mood. But Gena's mind was elsewhere anyway (and sex with Warren wasn't always the greatest, but then, that's normal, isn't it?), and she didn't sleep really well, because her thoughts were spinning, spinning, with all the things there were to do!

Chapter Eleven

She'd barely set her latte on the desk, and she hadn't yet put down her bag or hung her jacket on the hook behind her when Selma poked her head around the door.

"Marge wants to see you the minute you get in. She left a note."

There it was, in thick black ink. Marge Webster's imperious scrawl.

My office. ASAP!!

—MW

Uh oh! Am I in trouble?

"Did she look mad?"

"Well. Yeah. I guess so."

Gena dropped her bag and her jacket in a heap on her desk next to the Starbucks cup and headed right back to the elevator. A command from the editor in chief needed to be obeyed instantly. Especially when it came with double exclamation marks. On the way up to the forty-ninth floor, Gena reviewed her life and her work, found herself blameless on all scores, and decided that if Marge Webster was mad, it wasn't because of anything she had done.

Marge's door was closed, which was not a good sign. Gena squared her shoulders, took a deep breath, and knocked. From behind the door, she heard, "Yes!?"

That didn't sound friendly.

She opened the door, stepped in, and said, "Morning, Marge. You wanted to see me?"

With a gesture, Marge indicated the chair opposite her and didn't wait for Gena to get herself perched on its edge before she said, "Did you know Dinah was leaving?"

"What?"

"Dinah. Dinah Featherington. Did you know she was leaving?"

Gena was speechless. Her blank expression was answer enough.

"Just like that," Marge said, obviously angry. "Left a resignation letter here on my desk this morning and cleared out. Without a word of warning. No explanation. She said nothing to you?"

"She didn't say anything to me about leaving. I had no idea."

"I don't know how she could have just skipped like that, without a word to anyone. I hadn't a clue. *So* unprofessional! And all the features people are in turmoil now. Your whole department is in a stew."

"Whatever I can do, Marge. Of course."

"Good. Because I need you to pick up immediately on something Dinah was working on. Where are you on the Romy deVere piece?"

"I was up there, in Connecticut, on Friday. The interview went really well. She was great, and the story may have an interesting twist to it—"

"Whatever it is," Marge interrupted her, "you'll need to set it aside for a couple of days. Dinah had an interview set for this afternoon with Sonny Gaile at his home in Tennessee."

"Sonny Gaile? I'm seeing that kid everywhere these days. I didn't know Dinah was doing a piece on him."

"We'd just decided on it the other day. And he was able to squeeze us in for an interview this afternoon. You're going to fly down there today." She paused a moment to let Gena absorb this sudden shift in her plans for the day.

"Kind of sudden, Marge. But sure. I can rearrange some things. The deVere story can wait a bit."

"Good. The travel department made the necessary changes. Jerry Brewster got the ticket in your name. And he's put together all Dinah's material for you. You can review her notes on the plane. You should be able to make it to LaGuardia by 10:30."

"He's just a kid, isn't he? Is he even eighteen?"

"He's nineteen, and he's the hottest new thing on the country music scene these days. The kids are crazy about him. He's got a house in the woods, near some little town in the Smoky Mountains. That's where he grew up. Dirt poor. It's a real rags-to-riches story. It's all in Dinah's notes." The phone on her desk started ringing and she glanced at the ID. "I've got to take this," Marge said, picking up the phone. "And you better get moving if you're going to make it to LaGuardia to catch that plane." She waved Gena away, signaling their meeting was done, and turned her attention to the call.

At the door, Gena turned and mouthed a "thank you" to Marge, who nodded abstractedly. Gena was dismissed.

Outside, Dinah's assistant, Jerry Brewster, was waiting for her, with a folder of handwritten notes, a sheaf of article and photo printouts, and the flight confirmations.

"Did you know?" she asked as she took everything from him. "About Dinah leaving?"

"Not a word," he said. "You are so lucky," he said. "I want to hear all about him when you get back. Sonny Gaile! He's just the cutest thing!"

"I know, I know. But jeez—I better run. I've got one hour to get to the airport. And I've got to stop at home, make some arrangements."

As she hurried to the elevator, Jerry called after her, "Sonny's publicist will meet you at the airport." And as the elevator door closed, Jerry's voice trailed after her, "You're flying into Knoxville."

In her office, she retrieved her bag, her jacket, and the latte, and on the way down to the street, she was already calling Viv.

"Viv, omigod! I've got such a favor to ask."

"What's up?"

"Marge Webster is sending me to Tennessee in"—she glanced at her watch—"in fifty minutes. Our features editor quit without a word of warning, and I'm going in her place to some little town in the Smoky Mountains to interview Sonny Gaile! Of all people."

"Sonny Gaile?! Omigod! That kid is the very latest thing on the teen circuit! Making a fortune, I hear. That's so great. I can't wait to hear all about it."

"Well, yeah. But the thing is, there's Wiley."

"Wiley?" Viv had to think for a few moments. "Oh. Of course. You have a dog now."

"Right. I can't just leave him. And he and Warren don't get along at all. Not at all. Warren can't stand him, and he's been real clear"—At this moment, a taxi pulled over in response to Gena's waving arm—"*real* clear," she said as she got in, "that he refuses to have anything to do with him. I can't ask him to take care of Wiley. I think he'd rather let him starve." To the driver, she said, "Two Twelve East Seventy-Third Street," and to Viv she continued, "I bet he'd call someone to take him away rather than walk him—or let him mess in the apartment. So listen, Viv. I really need your help. Your studio is just a couple of blocks from my place. Please,

please, Viv. Can you meet me at my apartment right away—I'm on my way there now—and please take Wiley? Just till I get back. I haven't even had a chance to look at the notes or the itinerary, but I think I'll be back late tonight. No one said anything about another day. Please, Viv. I can give you everything. His food. His collar and his leash, and—"

"Of course, Gena. I can be there in a minute. Don't worry. Don't worry at all. Wiley will be in good hands. In fact, I'm looking forward to meeting him. Glad to have the chance. But you better be ready to tell me everything about Sonny. With pictures."

Gena sat back into the taxi's beat-up leather seat. Tons of tension fell off her.

"Viv. What would I do without you?"

She didn't know what Viv was thinking.

But this is what Viv was thinking:

Of course I'll help out. But Gena, honey, this could have been the crisis that would have forced you to dump that loser you're stuck with.

But what Viv said was: "It's a good thing my studio is close to your place. I'll run right over there. See you in ten."

Chapter Twelve

It was a whirlwind day and a half. Starting with a quick flight into Knoxville. She'd tried to call Warren before takeoff, but he'd cut her off sharply. "Can't talk now. Text me." That was all. He'd hung up before she could say a word. He'd been frosty at breakfast, probably still a little put-off after last night, and she'd hoped to mollify him with a chatty little call to let him know she'd be away for the day—maybe even a couple of days. Maybe he'd be impressed that she was on her way to Tennessee to meet with Sonny Gaile. After all, *everyone* wanted to meet Sonny Gaile! Also, she was eager to share with him the office news about Dinah's mysterious resignation, and to wonder with him what that could be all about. No one leaves *Lady Fair* for no good reason, and certainly not like that, without a word of warning.

But that was too much for a quick text message, and it was time to buckle up and turn off phones, so all she wrote was:

> *Have 2 b away—back tonite*
>
> *or maybe tmrw. on a plane*
>
> *2 Tennessee. Interviewing*
>
> *SONNY GAILE!! YAY ME!*

Then she put her phone away and got out the folder of Dinah's notes. There were articles about Sonny and his music, photos of his new home in the woods, some bio details, including a bit—but not much—about his childhood. Most of it was familiar—Sonny Gaile was too big a sensation for Gena to not be already aware of the usual publicly available information, including his relationship with Tim Fine, his producer, the man he credited with all his success. There was also a note, written in big, black, block letters on the last page of Dinah's handwritten notes: "**LISTEN AGAIN TO SONNY'S PERFORMANCE OF 'YOU ARE SO BEAUTIFUL.' FABULOUS!!!**" And then, underneath, "On YouTube. Concert 2 months ago, in London."

Gena had heard this performance. It had been all over the Internet when Joe Cocker died. But she made a mental note to hear it again.

* * * *

Sonny's publicist was waiting at McGhee Tyson. She was a tall blonde with gleaming teeth, spike-heeled knee-high boots, and a warp-speed style. Her name was Brittney Brisken, and she was all polite attention and enthusiastic, take-charge command as she whisked Gena away in Sonny's SUV to his "cabin" in the woods. Some cabin! Eighteen rooms, including a fully functioning, state-of-the-art recording studio, on a hundred and eighty acres of beautiful rolling hills.

Sonny turned out to be a sweet boy. Not at all the self-important, self-absorbed narcissist she feared the teen sensation would be. He was fair-haired and delicate of feature, with misty, gray-blue eyes that seemed to be looking into some remote other world. A fairy land, perhaps. He greeted her with genuine deference, plainly eager to be worthy of her time and of *Lady Fair*'s interest. He showed off his new home, entering each room—even opening closets and built-in cabinets and drawers—with an air of wonder, as though he wasn't sure it really was all his, had been built just for him.

"The architect went over every spec and every design idea first, and I did approve it all, but still," he said with a kind of awe-filled amazement. "I just don't get that I can have all of this now. And just for singing my songs. No one ever needed to give me a thing for singing. I sing because I'm alive. It's the only way I know how to *be* alive."

Gena was sure this was not posturing. His sincerity and innocence were apparent. She had her recorder going and was following him everywhere, taking notes like mad and using her cell phone camera to record everything.

After the full tour of the "cabin," he was concerned that she hadn't had lunch, and he called in his houseboy—yes, a *houseboy!*—and told him to tell the cook—a *cook*, too!—to make some sandwiches and coffee.

"Will that be okay?" he asked her. "Just sandwiches? Mrs. Wilkins is a whiz in the kitchen, but she wasn't expecting a guest for lunch, so I'm figuring it's not polite to toss a surprise at her. When we got a call from Dinah Featherington last night that she wouldn't be coming, we canceled our plans to go into town for lunch—Dinah and Brittney and me and Tim—and told Mrs. Wilkins to just leave us some sandwiches in the fridge. Then, just a little while ago, someone at *Lady Fair* called and said you'd be coming instead, so Brittney went hightailing it up to Knoxville to meet you. Tim is down at the barn with the horses, but I called him and said to get on up here so we can all have lunch together."

Gena said that would be very nice.

And she said she was looking forward to meeting Tim Fine. When he arrived, she recognized him from the photos. He was older than Sonny by about ten years, and they'd met when Tim, a music producer, had found Sonny tucked away in the foothills of the Smokies. He'd recognized his talent and turned him into a mega-star. The affection between the two men was apparent.

The introductions were made. Brittney, who had gone into the office to take care of some work while Gena got the tour, joined them for lunch, and then it was a visit to the horse barn, an imposing structure not like any barn Gena had ever seen. This was more like a small hotel, with stalls for eight horses and a fully furnished apartment upstairs for the groom, Linus, who, when they arrived, was in the wash bay, bathing one of the horses. The animals were indeed very beautiful, all gleaming black and proud and perfect specimens of their breed. Sonny walked along the stalls, greeting each horse, being nuzzled by them.

Gena was impressed. "Your horses really are beautiful," she said. "And they'll make wonderful pictures in the article."

"You should show her Belinda," Brittney said to Sonny, laughing. And to Gena she added, "Sonny thinks Belinda is beautiful, too."

"There's all kinds of beauty, Brittney," Sonny said. And to Gena he said, "Come on. Let's go meet Belinda. Brittney is always making fun of her, but yeah, I do think she's beautiful."

And Gena followed him out to the pasture behind the barn. Sonny whistled. And from the far side of the pasture, a horse came loping over to them. This was no gleaming black beauty. Big, she was, though. Ungainly big. And with the weirdest coloring and markings Gena had ever seen on any horse—even on a fantasy horse. For one thing, Belinda looked as though whoever made her couldn't decide if she was brown or black and white. Her front half was the color of caramel. But from her withers back, all the way over her rump and down her hind legs, she was painted in great, swirling swaths of black against white. Or maybe it was the other way around. She looked like a Native American blanket. For a horse, Belinda looked decidedly undecided. In addition, her mane was golden and her tail was gray.

"She's so *tall*," Gena said. "I'm just a city girl and I don't know horses, but your Belinda looks awfully tall to me."

"I think she may have some Percheron in her," Sonny said. "Percherons run pretty tall." Belinda nuzzled Sonny's neck fondly and he stroked her muzzle. "But she is so beautiful to me," he said. "Look at that sweet face. Look at the way she looks at me, with those beautiful eyes. She knows I love her." Belinda put her head on Sonny's shoulder and he stroked her soft cheek. "There isn't another horse on this earth that looks like my Belinda. She is absolutely all herself, not an imitation or a type. She doesn't conform to any standard. She's just proudly herself. And isn't that beautiful?"

* * * *

Brittney drove her into Merryville, a fifteen-minute drive away, where *Lady Fair*'s travel people had booked a hotel room for her. Over a couple of drinks in the hotel's tidy little restaurant, the two women worked out a plan for *Lady Fair*'s crew to come down to Tennessee to do a photo shoot, a plan that wouldn't conflict with Sonny's tour schedule. And they agreed to meet in the morning at nine so Sonny could show her his childhood home. They'd have her at the Knoxville airport in time for her two-thirty flight and she'd be home by five.

"And now," Gena said, "tell me more about that horse. Belinda. She's so weird looking, and Sonny seems to love her so much. I have a feeling there's a story there."

"No. No story, really. She's just the first horse Sonny ever owned. He's had her since he was a kid, and he just loves her. He was about fourteen, fifteen, and feeling like there was no future for him—you know, the way we all feel when we're adolescent, all confused and bleak—and he was walking in the woods, and there she was. She just came out of nowhere, pretty thin and ragged, with nothing to show where she belonged, and she just attached herself to him. And he took her home and cleaned her up and fed her, and I guess she's his friend the way only an animal can be. Sonny had a pretty hard life growing up, and he needed a friend, and I guess Belinda became that friend. I think somehow she gave him the confidence to let his singing be heard. And he thinks she's the most beautiful thing in the world. Maybe because he loves her. I guess that's it. If you love something, then it's beautiful. That's all. You can hear that in his music. When he sings about love, he's singing about something that's beautiful." Brittney picked the mint sprig out of her drink and nibbled on it. "Have you ever heard that concert performance he did in London? It was all over the Internet at the time."

"I remember," Gena said. "You Are So Beautiful."

"That's the one."

"I plan to listen to it later on tonight, after I have dinner. Dinah Featherington had it highlighted in her notes."

"Then you're all set. That's all you'll need. I have to leave you now. It's three o'clock on the coast, and I have calls to make."

"And I'll have dinner and then review what we did today."

"Ciao."

"Bye, now."

* * * *

The room they'd booked for her was clean and quiet, and Gena realized she really did need to gather her wits. What a day it had been. But first off, she had to call Warren.

Wait till he hears what a day I've had!

Her head was full of Sonny's "cabin in the woods" and the horses. The moment she heard Warren's voice, the excitement poured out.

"Oh, Warren. What a day! Sonny Gaile is a doll. He really is. So much nicer than I expected, and so much more interesting."

Warren said nothing for a moment. Then he said, "Who's Sonny Gaile?"

Now Gena had to pause, surprised, before she said, "I texted you."

She could tell he was trying to remember.

"Oh, yeah," he said. "Yeah, I saw it. I forgot. I've been busy. Tied up all day and I forgot you were away. You texted you were going to Tennessee. And who's this Sonny Gaile you had to see?"

"I thought you knew. Everyone knows who Sonny Gaile is."

"Never heard of him."

She was a little deflated. "You could have Googled him."

"C'mon, Gena. I have a life."

"He's the latest rage in country music. Everyone's listening to him."

"Not quite everyone. I never heard of him."

"*Lady Fair* sent me to do an article on him. He's a big deal, and it's a big deal for me, getting to do a story on him. And I've had such a great day, so exciting, and all day I wished you were here with me to share it. Let me tell you—"

"Listen, hon. I'm with some guys from the office right now, having dinner. Now's not a good time. When are you getting back?"

"I told you, in my text. Tomorrow. Maybe late afternoon."

"And you'll be with this Sonny guy?" She could hear how uninterested he was.

"Like I said. You could Google him."

Warren didn't even pick up on her irritation.

"Nah, I'll leave the country-boy research to you. You have time for that stuff. Just one thing, though. Do you think you could get yourself back here by six tomorrow night? There's a thing at Manish's house. The Parikhs are having a little party, just a few couples, and I said we'd be there."

Manish Parikh was Warren's branch manager, and Gena knew it was important to Warren to get an invitation like this. And she liked the Parikhs. Good people.

"I don't know, Warren. I'll try, but it'll be close. You know I'll try."

"Yeah, well, you do that. This matters to me."

"Of course, Warren."

"Listen, Gena." She could practically feel his impatience through the phone. "I gotta go," he said. Then he was gone.

And Gena held a dead connection in her hand.

She stared at the phone till the screen went black.

Then she turned it back on and found the YouTube video from London, the one that went viral last year, and she listened to young Sonny Gaile's remarkably mature performance of the classic song.

* * * *

Sonny arrived while Gena was having her pancakes and sausages. "Brittney's got herself tied up with some client in London," he said. "She'll catch up with us later and get you to the airport in time for your flight. Anyway, she's seen it all before."

He slid into a chair at her table and nibbled on a breadstick from the buffet.

"Is it a long drive to your old home?"

"No. It's just about five miles up the road. You probably didn't notice, but you passed it on the way to my place yesterday."

He was a little slumped in his chair, and he didn't look comfortable.

"Are you okay with this, Sonny?"

'No, it's okay. I said I'd do it. So I'll do it."

Gena remembered that there hadn't been much in Dinah's notes about Sonny's childhood. Just a scrawl at the top: "rags-to-riches." And "big family." And "be gentle."

Gena stood up and got her stuff together.

"Well, then. If you're ready, I'm ready. Let's go."

* * * *

It wasn't more than ten minutes away. Sonny pulled the SUV off to one side of the road and stopped there. "This is it," he said. "This is where I grew up." He had stopped in a weedy sort of clearing, an overgrown and ragged-looking space. Set farther back from the road, maybe thirty feet, in the shade where the trees were gradually encroaching, there was a house. Or, at least, there were the remnants of a house. More like a shack, actually, maybe a single room, not more than two. It had been painted white, once, a long time ago, but time and weather had flaked off most of its paint. A sagging door, broken windows, a couple of steps fallen from its front—and no sign of life. A casual passerby might have thought it was an abandoned storage shed or an animal shelter.

Sonny got out of the car and Gena came around to join him. He stood with his hands stuck into the back pockets of his jeans and stared at the place. For a long time he said nothing. Then, finally, after a deep sigh, he said, "This was my home, Miss Shaw. This is where I grew up."

"Is it okay to go in?" Gena asked.

"Sure," Sonny said. "I own the place now."

The shack turned out to have a main front room and a second smaller room to the back. Along one wall, there was a small, scratched-up, old-fashioned kitchen table of cream-colored metal with a flower design along the edge and two wooden chairs. There was a cast-iron cookstove to one side and a big tub with a large plank of wood over it for a countertop, but no sign of running water. There was a big bed in the back room and a sleeping loft with two mattresses—one for the boys and one for the girls. And a moldy, sour smell over everything.

"How many of you were there?" Gena asked.

"There was my ma and my pa and seven of us kids. I'm the oldest."

"Where are they now?"

Sonny's face lit up. "I been able to get them a new place, over by Merryville. A real nice house, with running water and indoor toilets and everything. And a big kitchen for Ma, and enough bedrooms so the boys can sleep separate from the girls. Growing up, we all went to school over in Merryville, but now they don't have to wait for a school bus to come and take them. Close enough now they can walk. Long as people like my music, there'll be enough money so they all have proper clothes and shoes and everything they need."

Then Sonny spoke very quietly, not looking directly at Gena. "The thing is, Miss Shaw, I've been interviewed a lot this last year or so, but I didn't feel right about letting people know this much about where I come from. No one's ever been to this place with me, before—no writer, that is, no reporters or people from TV. Truth is, I haven't wanted them to see it. Or to know that much about me.

"But I decided, finally, that it isn't right to hide it. There's plenty about where I grew up that people should know, and when that other lady, Ms. Featherington, called about a story for *Lady Fair*, I decided the time was right and I was ready.

"So here's the thing, Miss Shaw, you gotta write in your story that we had a lot of good stuff growing up here. The air is clean—not like in the big cities—and there were the birds in the morning to wake us up, and the sound of the wind in the trees. And being so close in this small place, and sleeping together in one bed, we had to get along. We had music, we had each other—and we had good parents who wouldn't let us be anything but good people. So this home, this little ramshackle place, was a happy home. And that's what I want you to write. The truth. You understand? Because there's beauty here. Lots of beauty. And I want you to look around"—here Sonny gestured around the flaking, decrepit, two-room shack—"and I want you to see that there's beauty here. And I want you to write about that."

Chapter Thirteen

*At the airport. Boarding soon. Been great. Can't
wait 2 tell u all about it.*

C U at home. Or at Parikhs if after 6.

Dress up. Where's the dog? With U?

Of course not. With Viv.

Gena added a few happy emoji. She was feeling great; her head was full of great story ideas, and all was right with the world. Sonny had spent an hour with her sitting at the kitchen table, and he'd shared with her the story of the life that had carried him from the shack along the side of the road to the so-called cabin on his one hundred and eighty acres of rolling countryside. It had been a fascinating morning, and it would be a fascinating story to tell on the pages of *Lady Fair*.

A tie-up on the Grand Central Parkway delayed her trip from LaGuardia back to East Seventy-Third Street. The apartment was empty but there was a note on the kitchen counter:

Couldn't wait. See you at the Parikhs.

Try not to be too late.

Viv called. She'll bring the dog back then.

She and Dan will be at the party.

* * * *

The mood at the Parikhs' home matched Gena's mood: high energy and good cheer. It wasn't a large group, just a few couples, including Viv and Dan, who'd been friends with Stephanie and Manish Parikh before Warren had even joined the firm. Glasses were tinkling and music was playing quietly and the conversation was convivial without being boisterous. Manish was seeing to it that everyone's glass stayed full and Stephanie was being her usual simple-but-elegant self, attending to everyone and being sure everyone was having a good time. When Gena arrived, Warren and Manish were deep in a discussion about the latest interest rate swap they'd negotiated, and Stephanie had just joined the group gathered around the coffee table, bringing with her a platter of shrimp. Dan and Viv were together on the sofa and waved Gena over. And Manish, when he saw that Gena had come in, nodded to Warren that they should join her.

"Glad you finally made it," Warren said to her as he pulled up a chair to join the group. And under his breath, "What took you so long?"

Gena just shrugged. She didn't think she was so late. Half an hour for an open-ended, casual party like this?

"Well, don't *you* look great," Viv said as Dan scooted over to make room on the sofa. "You're absolutely glowing. What's up?"

"Warren said you were away on an assignment," Dan said.

"Yeah," Warren said. "Some country singer I never heard of."

Dan spooned a bit of cocktail sauce onto his plate and dipped a shrimp into it. "Who?"

"Oh, Dan. Wait'll I tell you. Not just 'some singer.'" She got a napkin settled on her lap. She preened a little. She knew she was showing off, but it felt so exciting to be saying it. "I have just flown down to Tennessee to spend a couple of days with..." She paused to let the effect build up. "With Sonny Gaile!"

"Wow!" Dan turned to look at her admiringly. "You didn't! Oh, good for you, Gena. Sonny Gaile!"

"I never heard of him," Warren repeated.

'What do you mean," Dan said to Warren, "you never heard of him? Never heard of Sonny Gaile? What planet have you been living on?"

"Big deal. I never heard of him. So sue me!" Warren looked irritated. "I don't listen to country music."

"Neither do I," said Manish, who was standing behind Warren, adding some more wine to his glass and enjoying the conversation. "But even I have seen his photos all over the Internet."

"Yes," said Dan. "Sonny Gaile is the latest phenomenon in musical heartthrobs. His name is everywhere. Even I know the name. And the face. Young kid. Nice looking. Where has your head been this last year?"

"My head has been busy doing my job, thank you. Not busy getting distracted by fluff."

Dan shook his head and turned back to Gena. "So what's he like? Tell us all about him."

"Yes, yes," Viv burst in. "You lucky thing. I want to hear everything. Is he as cute as his pictures? Did he sing for you? Did you get to see his home? Tell us everything. Start at the beginning."

"Okay, you guys. I'll tell you everything."

She was about to start, but Manish said, "First you must have some wine. Let me bring you a glass." In a few steps, he went to a sideboard, which had been put to use as a bar, poured a glass of wine, and brought it back to Gena. "You must have a proper wine to accompany your story," he said.

Gena acknowledged her thanks with a nod, took a sip, and then started.

"His publicist met me at the airport and drove me to his house. They call it a cabin—I guess because it's in the woods—but no cabin I've ever seen had eighteen rooms, including its own private, fully functioning recording studio. He took me all around the place. Well, not exactly 'all.' It's a hundred and eighty acres. But I did get to see his horses. His property is at the base of the Smoky Mountains, and you know—there's this sort of blue haze that floats around them, so they really are kind of smoky. A little mysterious, like being in a fairy tale. And very beautiful."

It was all still fresh in her mind, and as she described the beauty of the Tennessee hills and the mountains and Sonny's house and the elegant barn and the beautiful horses, she realized that she was already creating the story she was going to write. Part of her was enthusiastically sharing her adventure, but at the same time, her mind was beginning to shape the completed article on the page. So she talked about the vast fireplace in the living room and the view from Sonny's upstairs rooms, but she chose to say nothing about his other home, the two-room shack he'd grown up in, the home of his childhood. That, it seemed, should be saved until she could think about it more deeply, and write about it carefully, thoughtfully. But she did tell them about rolling hills that sloped away to an elaborate horse barn that was not like the red barns in her childhood picture books, and deep-green grass and Smoky Mountains that really were smoky, in a bluish haze out of which an artist could spin all sorts of fantasies. And she told them that she found Sonny Gaile to be a young man of talent and grace and decency, who had found in himself a voice that spoke honestly and beautifully, a young man who seemed quite naturally to understand important things, like beauty and responsibility and gratitude. And a young man who was trying to cope with the great fortune that had fallen on him quite unbidden.

"You really liked him, didn't you?" Viv said.

"Oh, yes, I did, Viv. I suspect everyone likes Sonny Gaile. I found him very likeable." She thought about it for a moment. "You know, Viv, what I think I liked about him was his ability to see beauty, even where it wasn't obvious."

She was thinking of Belinda.

I have to think about that horse. There's something special there, something to write about.

Warren was looking increasingly sour. "I don't suppose this boy wonder bothered to hit on you, did he? Or do guys like him already have enough gorgeous babes hanging around them?"

Gena was appalled. "He's *gay*, Warren."

"Everyone knows Sonny Gaile is gay. Jeez, Warren." Dan gave him a sharp look, as if to say *stop it!* And then, deflecting, Dan said, "Hey, Gena, that's so great. You're going to make a great story out of this. And it's exciting, getting to spend time with a famous guy like that. You see his picture everywhere you go, and you get to say, 'Oh, Sonny Gaile. Yeah. I know him. We're old friends.' And by the way, did you get his autograph?"

"Oh, Dan, don't be silly. Of course I didn't get his autograph."

"Just kidding. I think it's just super for you. This kind of thing is going to really build your career."

Viv said, "I'm going to be able to tell everyone I had dinner the other night with a friend who knows Sonny Gaile. Has been in his home and everything. Told me all about it."

"Yeah," said Warren. His tone was sharp and sarcastic. "In every exquisite detail."

There was a pause. Viv looked at Dan. Dan looked at Warren. Gena looked down into her glass of wine. Deflation wafted through her, and she regretted her bit of hubris, her eagerness to bathe in an unaccustomed place as the center of attention. And Warren had some more wine, like a man who was celebrating a score he'd just made.

Dan turned to Gena and, as though to wipe out what had just been said, said, "Tell me more about the horses. I've heard about Tennessee Walking Horses. They're show horses, aren't they? Very beautiful. They have an unusual gait, right?"

Viv put her hand on his and gave him a look that seemed to say, *I remember why I love you.* "Yes," she said. "I once saw a documentary. And they're associated especially with that part of the country, aren't they, Gena?"

"Yes, I guess so." The exuberance she'd brought to the table was gone. Briefly, she told them about Sonny's hopes for his horses to win prizes, though she found herself thinking, instead, about Belinda.

Warren used the change in the momentum to take over the conversation.

"We were just talking, before you got here, Gena, about this new project I'm heading." The attention went back to Warren. He leaned back expansively, beaming. He raised his glass. "So let's all drink a toast to that." And they each said, "That's great, Warren," and, "Here's to Blass Investments' wonder boy," and Gena said, "I'm really proud of you, Warren." And Warren was happy to have all the energy and attention back on him, and he spent the rest of the evening talking about his big plans for the new project.

But he was not so expansive as they walked back to their apartment. He walked quickly, as though he wanted to make it hard for Gena to keep up, and he barely responded as she made the usual small talk about their dinner, and about Dan and Viv who, she thought, were getting really serious about each other, and he had only a perfunctory nod for Alfie, who usually got a big "Hi, there," from Warren. And he was preoccupied all the way up in the elevator.

In the apartment, he turned on the light and saw Gena's carry-on standing where she'd left it when she'd come home, next to the coffee table in the living room. She'd taken out her laptop and left her handwritten notes on the sofa, meaning to look at them before she went to bed. He turned to Gena and said, "Honey, I hope you're not going to go on gushing to everyone about how you went to Tennessee and met this great country singer. You know, it's not exactly cool to be acting like a teenager, all gaga about some little celebrity."

"I didn't think I was gushing."

"Well, you were kind of sucking up all the air. Like, you know, not everyone is interested." He was taking off his tie, opening his shirt, heading into the bedroom and tossing his clothes onto the bed. He turned around and saw that Gena was still standing in the middle of the living room, just looking at him, and he went back to her and put his arms around her. "After all, honey, if I'm going to be moving up the executive ladder, I'm going to need you to be a little more sophisticated."

"I wasn't gushing."

"Okay. Okay. Whatever you say. I just felt a little embarrassed for you, and I have to be able to tell you what I'm thinking, don't I? We've always been open with each other—"

"It was a big deal for me, Warren. It was fun and it was exciting. And it's important to my career, just like your project is important to your career. Why should I have to shut up about it?"

Warren stroked her hair and held her closer.

"Hey, honey," he said. 'Don't get all upset. I wasn't saying 'shut up' or anything like that. Come on. Don't be mad. Let's just forget about it. I'll pour us a drink, we'll watch a little TV, get a good night's sleep." He gave her a kiss and went over to the bar, picked up a bottle of Scotch, and checked the contents. "We're practically out of Glenlivet," he said, holding up the bottle so she could see.

"It is important to me, you know."

"Sure it is," he said. He put down the bottle and went into the bedroom. "I'm going to go get ready for bed. Why don't you open up that nice Italian red we picked up last week? Let it breathe a little first. I'll pick out a movie, if you like. Or we can watch some TV."

Later that night, much later, in a darkness lit only by the moonshine through the tall glass windows—and by the light from the fridge—Gena was taking a carton of ice cream out of the freezer.

Warren had been asleep for a couple of hours, but Gena, who was usually a sound sleeper, had been unable to shake the vaguely uneasy feeling she had—a fleeting feeling that came and then disappeared before she could put her finger on it—an uneasy, negative feeling that made her very uncomfortable. She'd been having this feeling for a while now, maybe for the last six months, maybe even a year—this indistinct sense of uncertainty, as though something wasn't quite firm beneath her feet. She seemed to be not liking herself. It was an awful feeling, especially because she couldn't figure out what was causing it. And this was the first time the feeling was strong enough to keep her awake.

But she'd learned long ago that ice cream would make her feel better.

Lucky Gena: She had the metabolism of a hummingbird and nothing ever packed fat onto her long, lithe frame. So there she was, at the fridge, taking out a carton of Caramel and Sweet Cream Coconut. She closed the door, got a spoon out of the drawer, and in the dark she crossed the living room and went to the deep ledge at the window that looked out over the nighttime view of the bridges over the East River. The little niche was fitted with cushions, and she settled in with her spoon and her ice cream and her uneasy and fitful insomnia.

"This can't be good," she whispered into the night across the window's glass. "I had such a good day, and I was feeling so good. And now I feel so down. Like I'm ashamed of myself. I don't know what I did." She was slowly spooning the ice cream from around the edges, where it was gradually softening. "On the plane this morning, I felt like I'd had a gold star pasted into my scrapbook. I felt so on top of everything. So pleased with myself. With Sonny's feeling safe with me, willing to share things he'd kept private. I felt like a good reporter. I'd earned a subject's trust."

She kept spooning ice cream.

"Maybe that's the problem. Feeling pleased with myself. Feeling proud. You know what they say about pride, Gena," she said, scolding herself. "About how pride goes before a fall."

She was about halfway down the carton of ice cream.

And she wasn't feeling better yet.

"But still. I know I shouldn't feel bad. Because I really do my job well."

She told herself that was the last word. The bottom line. The final judgment.

She'd been sitting there for fifteen minutes and the world was still spinning in its orbit, the stars were still shining over Manhattan, even if it was impossible to see them, and the boat passing along the river beneath her was not the least bit interested in Gena Shaw, sitting there high up in her forty-first floor apartment, eating ice cream and feeling foolish.

She went back to the kitchen, capped the ice cream, and put it back into the freezer. She didn't feel *totally* better.

But ice cream always helps.

And, still in the dark, she went back into the bedroom, got into bed, and just as she slid off into sleep, she thought:

Oh, shoot. I've been so busy with Sonny, I forgot all about Romy. Have to get back to that story. Be sure to check on photo shoot for all. Talk to Marge about Romy. I wonder what Dinah's departure is all about. So much to do. Can't wait to start on the Sonny Gaile story. Can't wait to get to the office. Can't wait...

And she slept soundly till the alarm went off at seven.

Chapter Fourteen

Turned out Marge Webster was on her way to a show in Milan and would not be back till early next week, so there'd be no immediate discussions about the amazing Romy deVere. And Dinah was gone, so there really wasn't anyone for Gena to talk to. Except, of course, Romy herself. And, because the photo shoot was scheduled for the following week, that would be the time to talk, as part of the follow-up interview. In the meantime, she'd have to sit on this potential scoop without breathing a word to anyone. But imagine *Lady Fair* breaking a bit of news like this! Romy deVere, sultry beauty and much-married star, exposed in a real-life role as dramatic as anything Hollywood might have produced.

Gena was so eager to get started, it pained her to have to set it aside—and to keep quiet about it, too. Good thing she had plenty more on her plate. Sonny Gaile, to begin with. There were the cell phone pics she'd taken; she sent those over to the photo department with instructions to get that shoot set up. And a note to be sure to include the barn and the horses, with maybe a sidebar about the entry of Sonny's horses in the show in Shelbyville.

Then there was the careful review and organizing of her Tennessee notes and thinking through a catchy angle—and then the outlining of the story. No matter what Warren said, Sonny Gaile was a phenomenon and *Lady Fair*'s readers were going to get an understanding of him that went well beyond the conventional tabloid fantasies and Internet sound bites.

The next time she looked at her watch, it was just after three o'clock.

Wiley! Poor Wiley. All those hours alone, poor little guy!

He hadn't been walked since early morning, when Viv had brought him home. But Gena had put in a good day's work and decided she could safely check out for a few hours.

Hang on Wiley. I'm coming.

Maybe she could telepathically get a message to him that she was on her way.

Be there in twenty minutes.

And she was. In twenty minutes, she was being greeted by a prancing, tail-wagging little bundle of pure excitement. His delight in seeing her made her heart sing, and right then and there she joined a very special society: the very fortunate club of people who know the joy of coming home to unconditional and exuberant love. As she knelt to attach Wiley's leash to his collar, he seemed to be unable to get close enough to her, licking her face, rubbing his cheek against hers, pawing at her chest. If his long, skinny legs were arms, he would certainly have wrapped them around her.

"Okay, okay!" She was laughing as she struggled with his wriggling body to get him ready to go out. "We're going, we're going. You'd think I'd been away for a month."

By the time the elevator carried them down forty-one floors and they'd gone through the lobby and out onto the street, Wiley was pulling hard on his leash with much greater strength than she'd have thought such a small dog could have, desperately eager to get to the nearest tree. Which was, of course, bad city-dog manners but neither Wiley nor Gena had yet been schooled in the ethics of public-toilet protocol for dogs. Wiley had spent his young life in the country and Gena had never paid attention to dog life in the city. They both had much to learn. But the day was lovely and she had put her work behind her, so she could now indulge in a leisurely walk around the neighborhood, enjoy a little window-shopping, pick up a bottle of Glenlivet for Warren, maybe walk over to the park. She might decide to buy an ice cream and sit on a bench, where she and Wiley could do some quiet people-watching. A lovely day in New York.

Madison Avenue was gleaming in the afternoon sunlight. Everything seemed newly washed and freshened up, as though it was expecting an important visitor. What a pleasure it was to just stroll, to notice other dog owners and their pets, perhaps to nod to them, or even pause for a moment while the dogs explored each other, to take the time to enjoy the clothes in the elegant shops, to examine the restrained displays in the windows of drugstores so upscale they called themselves "apothecaries," to imagine having the wealth it would take to buy one of the apartments being offered for sale in the windows of the local real estate agent. To consider buying a bunch of flowers for no reason at all.

Gena had no reason to buy a bunch of flowers. But Wiley had pulled her over to a display banked up against the front of a produce store, and she felt drawn to their fresh, colorful cheeriness. For a while, she contemplated a purchase, trying to think of a reason. It wasn't a holiday. Neither she nor Warren was having a birthday. She wasn't sure, even, if between them they owned a vase. If she bought them, what would she put them into?

While Gena considered all this, Wiley was making friends with a small, silky white dog whose owner had come up beside her. Gena looked down at the dog and had an instant memory of a scent, the scent of a Cartier perfume. La Panthère. Could this be Sweetie Pie, the Crested owned by Harriet van Siclen? Mrs. van Siclen, who was on her way to Australia? There had been a brother, a brother who was too busy to talk, who dashed past her, barely noting her existence. What was his name? She remembered only a tall man silhouetted against a window, talking on his phone. This man standing next to her was the same man. But now, he was not in a rush. He was now looking at her closely, with his head tilted a bit, as though this were more than a chance encounter.

"It's Paul," he said. "Paul Brackman. You were at Harriet's place the other day," he said. "You're the writer. With the hairless dog. She told me about you." He looked down at Wiley. "And this must be the dog."

"Yes, this is Wiley. I didn't think you noticed me."

"Oh, yes. I noticed you."

His expression was—what was it? She couldn't quite read it…satisfied? Yes, that was it. He looked satisfied. How odd.

"I remember," Gena said. "You were on the phone. And you were in a hurry."

"I may have been rude. I'm sorry."

"No, it's all right. Everyone's in a hurry these days. We're all so busy. And things were—well, sort of frantic that day, what with the packing and the rush and everything—"

Gena was remembering what she'd noticed that day—that he was good looking, in a grown-up, sedate sort of way, and that she'd wished he hadn't been in such a hurry.

"Yes, it was pretty frantic. Harriet was so distracted that day, she couldn't remember your name. Only that you were writing something about dogs. Did you get everything you needed?"

"For the time being, I think. But there's so much to learn. I've never had a dog before."

"Maybe I can help. We're dog people, and this is a breed our family has had for some years. Three sisters, they all have Cresteds."

By now, they'd both forgotten about flowers and were walking together up Madison Avenue.

"My immediate problem," Gena said, "is what to do with him all day. I hadn't realized, if you have a dog, you can't just leave him alone all the time. I was out of town for a couple of days this week and my friend took him till I got back last night, but she's busy, too, and that's not a permanent solution. He's a lively little thing, and I can see that he needs to get out more, he needs to run and play."

"Absolutely."

"That's why we never had any pets. My dad thought it was wrong to keep a dog cooped up all day in a city apartment. He said dogs should have a chance to run freely, that they need the exercise. So I can bring him out to walk him, but that's not enough, is it?"

"No, of course it's not. It's always a problem for city people who work all day. You could hire a hire a dog walker. That works well for some people, and the dog gets to be with other dogs, which is good for his social life."

"But then the person you hire has to have access to your apartment when you're not at home. I'd be uncomfortable with that."

"You might consider day care. I take Sweetie Pie to East Side Dog Prep and Day Care. It's nearby, over on Seventy-Ninth Street, near Sutton Place. They have veterinarians on call, and their staff is excellent. They take only small dogs, and you have to provide all the dog's papers, latest medical records, proof he's had his shots."

"Sounds expensive."

"It is. But for emergencies, it may be a good choice. You should also check out the places in the park that are designated dog friendly. The closest one near here is right behind the Met." He gestured a couple of blocks away, toward the Metropolitan Museum of Art. "Dogs are allowed to be off-leash for three hours in the morning and three hours in the evening. The rest of the day, they're allowed in the park only on-leash. It's not enough, of course, but it helps."

She's been only partly listening to him.

He has such a nice face. Intelligent and engaged. He's actually paying attention to me. Nice gray eyes. Great haircut, and the barest touch of gray at the temples. Maybe late thirties? Not older, I think.

"That's good to know," she said. "This is a totally new experience for me. And my boyfriend is no help. He hates Wiley, and Wiley barks his head off whenever Warren gets close to me. I don't know what we're going to do about him."

"Ah." Paul looked at her thoughtfully. "You have a boyfriend."

He said nothing for a long moment. Then he looked at his watch as though he'd just remembered a previous engagement. Or something. "I am sorry, it seems I'm always rushing off somewhere. I have a meeting downtown and I need to get the Pie to her day care. I hope you and Wiley work it out with your boyfriend. Cresteds are great dogs, and I hope you'll be happy with this one."

He turned east toward Park Avenue, said a brief goodbye, and Gena watched him and Sweetie Pie until they disappeared around the corner.

"That was odd," she said to Wiley. "Maybe I shouldn't have mentioned Warren."

Wiley gave her a look that said, "You think?"

Chapter Fifteen

She saw him again, late on Saturday night. She and Warren had been to a movie and they were walking along Broadway opposite Lincoln Center, mingling with the after-theater crowd, when a cab pulled up in front of them and a couple got out. As the couple went into Café Fiorello, Gena recognized Paul. She also recognized the woman he was escorting into the restaurant: Cherie Blitz, gorgeous runway model, latest sensation from Germany. Her silvery hair was elaborately coiffed, her evening frock was a froth of haute couture in pale blue, and her strappy sandals were, at the very least, four inches of spike heel. Gena was accustomed to spectacular beauties—they were commonplace around *Lady Fair*. But she was surprised by the pang of jealousy that fluttered through her when she recognized Paul Brackman as Cherie's date. After all, what was Paul Brackman to her? Nothing. Why should she wish, even if only for a fleeting second, that she were in Cherie's place? She was ashamed of such an unworthy thought. She put her hand through Warren's arm and turned to look fondly at him—as he, in that same moment said, "Wow, some guys have all the luck!"

She saw that Warren's eye had also been caught by the attractive couple, only it wasn't Paul he was smirking at, of course: his attention was on Cherie Blitz, and his expression was almost predatory.

Gena took her hand off his arm and said nothing. There was that bad feeling again. She tried hard to ward it off, telling herself Warren's reaction was perfectly ordinary; any red-blooded grown man would want to be seen with a gorgeous woman like Cherie. Right? And she couldn't help it that she couldn't be that gorgeous woman. How many women could be so lucky? Beauty like that is rare, and it was certainly beyond anything she'd ever be able to achieve.

But later that night, as she took Wiley out for his last walk before bedtime, she confided in him. "Gee, Wiley. I wish men would look at me that way. I wish Warren would look at me that way."

Just hearing Warren's name was enough to get a response from Wiley. He lifted his leg against a hydrant, and Gena took that to be his opinion on the matter.

"I know, I know, Wiley. I know what you think of my boyfriend. But he has his good points. He works hard and he really wants to make something of himself. He's just getting more and more tied up in his work, trying to get ahead. The investment banking business is so demanding and there's so much stress—"

She knew she was just talking to herself, but it felt good to see how Wiley was attentive to her, as though they were having a real conversation.

And later, hours later, when she found herself again sitting in the niche by the window, spooning up gobs of ice cream, it was especially good that Wiley came and sat with her.

Chapter Sixteen

Not even six o'clock yet, and Warren was still sleeping. Gena slipped quietly out of bed, pulled on a pair of jeans and an old tank top, and stepped into her favorite moccasins. The old shoes were ragged after years of use, but she loved them, and they served her well when she was in a rush and feeling casual. She didn't stop to wash or brush her teeth, just raked her fingers through her hair to give it a semblance of order. On an early Sunday morning she could probably take advantage of the anonymity New York provided, and she would take the time to tidy herself up when she got back. She grabbed a doughnut out of the bread box, collected Wiley, and headed out for the park. Her destination was the off-leash area Paul had told her about, behind the Met. Wiley would be glad for a free run, and she could sit and gather her wits. It had been a restless night with not enough sleep, and an hour or two in the park would give her a chance to steady her mood before it was time for breakfast with Warren. It used to be that Sundays were lazy days, taking it easy, having the time for waffles or omelets, sharing sections of the Sunday *Times*, maybe deciding on a movie or getting together with some friends. But lately, Warren had been running off to play golf on Sundays, or he'd needed to be at the office where, it seemed, life ran twenty-four seven and no one ever said "no." He'd become so in love with his own ambition, and it seemed she wasn't able to keep up, not able to be what he thought he needed her to be now that he was moving up the corporate ladder.

But who could feel stressed on a quiet Sunday in the park? The trees seemed to whisper "There, there. Take it easy. Everything is going to be fine." And indeed, once she'd arrived at the dog-friendly space beyond the museum, she knew this was the perfect place to shed the unease that had been nagging at her. There were only a few dog people there, sitting on the benches, some chatting with each other, most of them reading the morning paper, almost all of them with a Starbucks coffee, either in their hands or set onto the bench next to them. Wiley took one look and knew he was in dog heaven. As soon as the leash was off his collar, he took off like a madman, racing at top speed to the far end and circling back again, back and forth, over and over. Those skinny long legs seemed to have been made for high-speed chases, and soon he was joined by a small Schnauzer, a Bichon Frise, and a scraggy-looking fellow of indeterminate parentage. Dogs at play were wonderful to watch, and Gena forgot herself and her frazzled mood as the dogs stopped their frantic running and began to play, climbing on each other, making little growling noises, acting fierce, like little boys being warriors.

A man's voice behind her. "They're fun to watch, aren't they?"

She knew the voice immediately. Her hand went to her hair, and she wished she'd taken a couple of minutes to brush it out properly—and dress a little less ragged.

"I like how easily they make friends," she said as Paul came around the bench and sat down next to her.

He had Sweetie Pie with him, and he bent to unleash her. He gave Pie a pat on her back and said, "Go ahead, Sweetie." And Sweetie Pie went off to explore on her own. "So you found this place. Good."

Odd, again. That look. Very subtle—very minimal—just something around the mouth—or was it his eyes?—a fleeting look of satisfaction. *They really are nice eyes...couple of crinkles at the edges. Mid-thirties,* she decided. *An older man. S*he laughed to herself. *And nice.*

"Yes. I'm glad I did. I can't believe how badly Wiley needed the exercise. Now he's playing with the other dogs. Making friends, I think. But you should have seen when we first got here this morning. He was racing around like a maniac."

"I did see him. I was here earlier and I saw you when you got here. And I saw how he took off the minute he saw green grass and his leash was off."

"You were watching us?"

"For a while. I hope you don't mind. I wasn't spying, you know. Just enjoyed watching you and Wiley. You're nice together."

She didn't know what to make of that. And she didn't know what to say. So she sat there silently and thoughtfully for a while. And then, impulsively, she said, "I saw you last night."

She was instantly embarrassed, and she stumbled over herself trying to make it sound natural. "You were with Cherie Blitz. On Broadway. You were getting out of a cab."

"She turns heads everywhere, of course."

"She certainly turned my boyfriend's head. He said he was jealous of you. Being with a beauty like Cherie."

"Ah. The boyfriend. He told you he was jealous. Of me?"

She nodded. "In so many words. What he said was, 'Some guys have all the luck.'"

"I'm sorry." He looked at Gena kindly. He seemed about to say something, but stopped himself. Then, after a pause, he said, "You can tell that boyfriend of yours he shouldn't be jealous. Maybe I'll meet him someday, and I'll tell him myself."

Something had gone a little harsh in those gray eyes.

They both sat silently for a moment or two, watching the dogs. Then Gena spoke.

"So is Cherie Blitz your girlfriend?"

He laughed. "Hardly. She's a client."

"Oh?"

"My firm is representing her. She needed an escort for an event last night. I volunteered."

"Not exactly hazardous duty, I think."

He laughed. "No, it was fun. Cherie is fun, it was a good evening, and I had a good time."

"Maybe my boyfriend is in the wrong business. He doesn't seem to have much fun in his work."

"The boyfriend again." His eyes got that harsh look again. "What's this boyfriend's name?"

"Warren. Warren Haglund."

"And what does he do?"

"He's an associate at Blass Investments. Just moved up from analyst."

"And ambitious, right?"

Gena sighed. "That's a good thing, isn't it?"

"In a way."

"And are you ambitious?"

"In a way. Not the same way. What about you?"

His question surprised her. Had she ever been asked before about her ambitions?

"I want to get really good at what I do," she said. "I want to make a difference. I'm working for a fashion magazine, and some people think that's all fluff and nonsense. Insignificant stuff. But first of all, I'm glad I've got the job. And second, I get to work with talented people, and *Lady Fair* has some of the best. And third, maybe most important, I have a chance to interview subjects whose lives have been out of the ordinary, subjects who make their dreams come true, or maybe who were hit with good luck—or even bad luck—and have managed to spin that flax of good or bad luck into the gold of success. I get to dig below the surface, below what the public thinks it knows about them, and maybe get to a deeper level. If I'm lucky. And if I'm skillful enough."

She stopped abruptly, realizing she was letting her passion for her work slip out and maybe seeming foolish. But Paul was looking at her with interest.

"And what are you working on now?"

She thought of her trip to Tennessee and Sonny Gaile—and then she remembered Warren's scolding her for her "gushing," and she put an immediate brake on her enthusiasm.

"There's a young country singer people are interested in right now. He's been kind of a sensation, and I'm doing a piece on him."

"Not Sonny Gaile, by any chance?"

"Actually, yes. I'm surprised you even know his name."

"Well, you said 'kind of a sensation' and I have been seeing his name around lately. So I'll ask the usual question: What's he *really* like? What did you think of him?"

Gena spoke with restraint, remembering again not to gush. "He's really very nice. Sweet. Sincere. Not phony sincere. You'll have to read the article when it's published."

"I will. I'll look forward to it."

"I'm also working on a piece about Romy deVere."

"My God, that's a name that goes back a long way. She was a big star when my parents were young. No, when my *grandparents* were young. Wasn't she considered the most beautiful woman in the world in her time? Married a bunch of times and sort of scandalous. Something of a femme fatale in her day, wasn't she? I didn't know she was still alive."

"Yes, she's the one, and yes, very much alive. And with a whole new career. At ninety-seven, that's pretty remarkable. She's been making some beautiful artwork, with showings in local galleries up in Connecticut. We think our readers will be interested in a woman who is "old," and yet "new." That there is life after white hair and wrinkles. What's on the outside doesn't tell you what's on the inside. And not only because she was famous and beautiful. Not for what she was, but for what she is now." Gena stopped. Her voice was rising and again her eagerness for her work was making her "gush." She made herself slow down. "Well, anyway. There's more to Romy deVere than people realize." She pursed her lips and, with an effort, stopped talking about her.

"You say that as though there are secrets there. Do you have privileged information?"

"I've said too much already."

"And I should just read the article when it comes out." He smiled genially.

"That's about it. I'm shutting up now." And she smiled, too.

Then they were both thoughtful. For a long time. Just watching the dogs. Until Wiley broke away and trotted back to Gena. At the same time, Sweetie Pie ended her explorations and also joined them. The two dogs acknowledged each other with the usual sniffings and tail waggings.

"I guess I need to be getting back. Almost time for breakfast. And I have work to do." Gena knelt to put Wiley's leash on. Paul bent to pick up Sweetie Pie. This brought Gena and Paul close together. She picked Wiley up. Then she and Paul stood up, still close to each other.

"You said Wiley was protective of you. Wouldn't let Warren get close." She nodded.

He stroked the back of Wiley's neck, and Wiley lifted his head for more. "You were worried that maybe Wiley has a problem?"

"I was. I am."

"There's nothing wrong with Wiley. He seems to be okay with me. Maybe Wiley knows something."

"What do you mean?"

"I'm not sure. But dogs are smart. I've learned to pay attention to their messages. You need to understand what they're telling you." He smiled at her. "Good luck with your stories. I'll look forward to reading them—and I'll be proud to say I know the woman who wrote them. I know they won't be ordinary puff pieces." He nodded, as a man might who was tipping his hat. "Have a nice breakfast. Maybe I'll see you here again. Our dogs seem to like each other." And then he turned and left, heading toward the park's Eighty-Fourth Street exit.

Gena turned to look into Wiley's face.

"You didn't mind him, did you? You let him pet you. You didn't bark and you didn't snap, did you? You sly dog."

Chapter Seventeen

"When does Marge get back?" Gena stopped Selma as she passed her coming out of Gena's office. As usual, Selma-the-intern was moving at top speed.

"Wednesday. And there's a message for you," Selma called back over her shoulder, "from someone named Brittney. I left it on your desk." And she disappeared around the corner.

"Thanks," Gena called after her.

The message on the desk was brief. "Hi, Gena. Can you keep a secret? Call me. Use your cell, not your office phone. Don't text." And there was a phone number—with a Los Angeles area code.

She put her coffee down, hung up her jacket, and stuck her bag in the bottom drawer of her desk.

She sat down. She read Brittney's message one more time. Then she got her cell phone out of her pocket and called Brittney's number.

"That's an intriguing message you sent," she said when Brittney answered. "What's up?"

"For some reason, Sonny really liked you."

Gena laughed. "That's because I'm so likeable."

"Well, actually, you are. I didn't mean that the way it sounded. I just meant that of all people, he's picked you, even though you've had only a couple of days' contact. Sonny could have given this story to any one of the thousands of media people in the whole world. And I mean: The. Whole. World. I don't know what it was about you, but apparently he really trusts you."

"Okay. Now I really am intrigued."

"This is absolutely off the record."

Gena laughed. "I figured."

"You have to absolutely promise."

"Brittney. You shouldn't even say that to me." She already had a yellow pad and pencil ready. "Of course. I promise. As long as it's nothing immoral, or illegal."

"Okay, okay. Here's the thing: Sonny and Tim Fine have decided to give *Lady Fair* this story. Exclusive! We want *Lady Fair* to break this news on its pages well after the event. The public will not know until the issue appears weeks from now. Can you guys keep a secret that long?"

"Brittney, I'm proud to say that *Lady Fair* has earned its reputation for honorable journalism. We're not a tabloid, and we value the trust our readers put in us." On the yellow pad in front of her, Gena tapped her pencil a bit impatiently. "Did you ever hear a word about Gaby Rider's pregnancy until we put that Axelrod photo of her showing off her *big* baby bump on our cover? That cover, and the story, were in preparation for weeks before we published it. And the collapse of the Gelson fashion empire? There'd have been repercussions on the stock market if we'd let that story leak before Gelson was ready to go public with it in our story last fall. He trusted us to keep it quiet until the agreed-upon time. And there are plenty more. There's a reason women—and plenty of men—read *Lady Fair*. We are about beauty, sure. But we're also about the truth. And you know what the poet said about truth and beauty."

Brittney laughed. "Gena, I'm British. Every British kid learns those lines of Keats's poem."

"Right. 'Beauty is truth, truth beauty—that is all ye know on earth.'"

"Beauty and truth are the same thing. You guys should have that on your masthead."

"We do."

There was silence for a moment or two while their exchange resonated between them. Then Brittney said, "Okay, Gena. Here's what I'm giving you: next Monday, the twenty-sixth, the day you'd set for the photo shoot, Sonny and Tim are getting married."

Gena's pencil was already flying. She'd tipped to the story the moment Brittney mentioned Sonny and Tim in the same sentence. *Good for them!* she was thinking.

"Monday," Brittney repeated. "It will be very quiet, a very private ceremony at Sonny's cabin. Tim's father got himself ordained as a minster and he's flying in from Oregon to perform the ceremony. I'll be there, of course, and you and I can be the official witnesses—if that's okay with you. And the camera crew can get the whole thing as part of the coverage they were going to do anyway. But you will have to promise me that they will be silent until the story appears. There will be the usual nondisclosure papers to sign, of course. But Sonny and Tim—and I—are trusting there'll be no leaks."

"Brittney, it's an honor. I am so flattered that Sonny and Tim put such trust in me, and in the *Lady Fair* people. You know we'll handle this with complete discretion."

"We're counting on you."

"I'll meet with our photo editor, and he'll handle the details with his crew from this end. I'll be in touch in the next day or two to coordinate with you. And please tell Sonny I send my congratulations to him, and to Tim. Best wishes to them both."

The conversation with Brittney lifted Gena's spirits several notches up from the low level they'd been dropping to lately. Not only was the vote of confidence by Sonny and Tim a nice personal pat on the back, but the scoop for *Lady Fair* would earn her some professional points with Marge Webster. And in the meantime, till Marge got back from Italy, she could move ahead on Romy deVere's story. She'd already set up the photo shoot in Connecticut for tomorrow, and had scheduled some extra time to spend with her subject to talk about the revelations her research had uncovered.

She sat back in her chair. She drank a few sips of her latte. She thought about secrets. *Seems there are secrets everywhere*, she thought. So many people have secrets. Romy. Sonny. So many public people—politicians, great artists, flash-in-the-pan celebrities, long-lost relatives. Close friends. There were secrets Viv had shared with Gena that Dan would probably never know about. And just as well.

The only secret Gena could think of in her own history was when she was seven and took a lipstick from a drugstore cosmetics display. It was a memory she returned to frequently. And again, as always, as she ran the mental tape of that memory, she corrected herself.

I didn't "take" that lipstick. I stole it.

She hadn't been caught, and to this day she hadn't told anyone. But it was always with genuine shame and remorse that she thought of her theft. She'd long ago stopped making excuses for that bit of bad behavior. Even though she'd come to understand that a single episode of shoplifting of some small item is a fairly common childhood event, and even though she could no longer remember the store or where it was located, and she knew that neither the national economy nor the republic itself had collapsed as a result of her tiny thievery, it was morally unacceptable, and she felt she was owed a punishment.

But, oh, even these many years later, she still experienced the almost hypnotic power of that luscious, creamy, smoothly perfect object of scarlet seduction. It had spoken to little Gena of "magic and power, of unlimited possibilities, of a world of excitement and dreams not even yet dreamed, of things to come—and yes, it spoke to her of beauty. She took it home and hid it under the scarf her grandmother had given her for Christmas.

She'd been disappointed that Grandma hadn't given her something to play with—a toy, or a doll, a board game, perhaps—but Grandma had said, "But you can play with it, dear. If you're careful not to damage it, you can play dress-up and pretend you're having tea with the queen." The scarf, with its multicolored sumptuousness in its ornately decorated box, was the perfect place to hide her illicit loot, and she slipped the gleaming black tube of fantasy under the silken fabric.

As she grew older, Gena did, indeed, often sit at the little vanity table in her bedroom and put on the lipstick and try out various ways to tie that scarf, to drape it dramatically about her shoulders, over her head, across her torso. Her dreams of loveliness were built on the luxury of the scarf and the excitement of the stolen lipstick, making herself "beautiful," acting out scenarios and dialogues that she imagined were grown-up and alluring. But sadly, this game of make-believe died away by the time she left junior high, as she was confronted with a more mature understanding of the mirror's reality.

By that time, she had reconciled herself to the inescapable truth: She was not beautiful. She was too tall, taller than the boys in her class. She was too thin, too thin to need a bra or to wear a bikini bathing suit. She was too sharp-elbowed to meet any conventional standard of femininity. Her charms, if she dared to call them "charms," were her journalistic talent, her willingness to listen to other people's life histories without feeling they needed to hear hers, and her scrupulous honesty. Except, of course, for her one tiny crime, for which she knew she should be sorry. With only one exception, she told no one, and kept it as the one secret in her life that she'd take to her grave.

The exception was Warren. Warren was special. They'd met in history class in their junior year back in high school. They'd sat next to each other, shared snide jokes about the teacher, criticized the subject matter, exchanged notes occasionally, and by the end of the semester had become casually friendly. Not more than that. Maybe a "hi" or a nod in the hallway. A meeting, perhaps, at the local fast food hangout, along with other classmates.

And then, for some unexplained reason and to her great surprise, Warren Haglund singled her out when it was time for the boys to take a girl to senior prom. He asked her and she said yes, and when he took her home, he kissed her good night. It was a real kiss, Gena's first, believe it or not, and when she went into her room—after a brief account of the evening to her mother, who had waited up for her—she took down the old, ornately decorated box, faded and scratched now, from the shelf at the top of the closet. The beautiful silk scarf had long ago been promoted to a place in her dresser drawer, but the lipstick, worn to a small nub, was still there. She took it to her vanity table, sat down, and put a light dash of red to her mouth, a mouth that had just felt, for the first time, a man's hunger. She took a very deep breath, as though she could pull that sensation, the memory of it, deep into herself, to save it forever, and she decided she was in love with Warren Haglund. She was seventeen years old. And ready, she was sure, to be a woman.

And that's how she came to tell Warren the secret of her youthful crime. One evening, in that first lovely time of *really* getting to know each other, she revealed, oh so timidly, the dreadful truth about her wicked adventure, so long concealed. And Warren laughed, and told her he'd done something similar but so much worse: At fourteen, he and some other guys stole a pack of condoms from a drugstore. Actually, one boy was a lookout and the others had created a diversion, "accidentally" knocking over a display case, eliciting much noisy attention from shoppers and salesclerks, while it was Warren himself, the designated thief, who took the packet from the from the rack and then ran like hell.

Warren laughed a lot as he told the story, and Gena laughed with him, but privately she wasn't so sure. It was still stealing, and she was sorry she'd told Warren about her bit of juvenile delinquency. The next day, she threw the lipstick away and she never mentioned the event again.

After high school, she and Warren went to different colleges, she to a small school upstate, where she majored in journalism, and Warren to NYU as a business major. They were in regular contact during those years, by phone and text mostly, and they spent all their time together when she came into the city for holidays and vacations. After graduation, Gena interned at a small local newspaper near her school, and Warren entered NYU's MBA program. By this time, they were a serious and regular couple, and when Gena came back to New York and took the job at *Lady Fair* they agreed to move in together. It seemed the natural thing to do. That was four years ago—almost five.

Almost five years they've been living together, never talking about marriage, somehow feeling marriage just wasn't a part of their future, and as she sat in her office, wandering down memory lane and wondering about the path ahead of them, she was aware of something secret happening inside herself. In her head? In her heart?

But her wandering and wondering were cut short. Ira Garlen from the art department needed some information about the Romy deVere shoot, and he arrived at Gena's office with a knock-knock on her open door and a breezy "Can I come in?" as he entered. And that was the end of Gena's thoughts about secrets and history and the future—at least for the time being.

Chapter Eighteen

The next day, when Gena needed to drive to Connecticut for the Romy deVere shoot, she had not yet been able to make arrangements for Wiley, and she couldn't bear to put him in a kennel, where he'd be caged like a criminal—poor little nervous guy would freak out, she was sure—so there was nothing to do but take him along. One other thing Gena knew she'd let slide: Dr. Zweig had explained that the law required her to make a good-faith effort to find Wiley's owner. While she hoped—fervently—that no owner would turn up to claim him, she knew she wouldn't be able to live with herself if she didn't try. So she bought a doggie car seat to strap onto the front passenger seat of her car, and she packed up his snake and his bowls and some kibble, and she made up a batch of "Lost Dog" flyers with Wiley's photo on them, packed the whole caravan into her car, and by seven o'clock on Tuesday morning, she was on her way to I-95 and Connecticut.

The drive to Romy's cabin would take almost three hours, and the plan was to meet up with the photo crew at noon. But she had an additional plan that had nothing to do with the photo shoot. When she'd driven as far as Shanesville, she located the local veterinarian, whose name she'd found through Google. Dr. Bettina McCarron was sympathetic but, no, there had been no reports of a lost dog of any kind, let alone a male hairless Chinese Crested. She had nice things to say about the breed, and was impressed that Gena was trying to find the owner. "Around here we deal mostly with livestock, large animals, horses and cows. A dog like your Wiley is a pure pet and in the cold winters we get up here, he might not be a very satisfactory one. Definitely needs special care—lots of sunblock even when it's not brilliant sunlight, and special little booties to fit over those skinny legs and long feet. And think how cold he'd be with no hair on him. He'd need a really warm coat to cover as much of his little body as possible."

From there, Gena stopped at the gas station, where a different empty-headed teenager looked blankly at her and said she could leave the flyer on the counter if she liked, but, no, he didn't hear nothing about no lost dog, but maybe she could ask at the diner down the road. Which she did. A nice, elderly, rather rustic-looking gentleman, who was sitting at the counter having a late breakfast, overheard her inquiry. He looked at Wiley's photo on the flyer, said he was sorry but he hadn't seen the dog, and then told her the following:

"Musta been about two weeks ago, that time we had three straight days of pouring rain, a family come in here, mom and daddy and three kids. They didn't have a dog with them, but I could tell they were talking about a dog. And the youngest kid, a little boy, maybe seven years old, kept saying, 'You said I could keep him. You did. You said.' And the daddy said, 'No way. I said when you found him, you could keep him while we were on our vacation, but no way was that dog coming all the way back to Moline with us. Funny looking thing he is, I'd be ashamed for the neighbors to see us with a weird dog like that.' And he told the kid to just put him out in the parking lot and someone would probably pick him up. And the kid was crying some, but I guess that's what he did. Too bad about that, leaving a little animal out in the rain all alone."

Well, you *certainly didn't do anything to save him.* Gena kept the thought to herself, but now the man didn't look so nice to her. *People can be full of compassion until it's time to get up out of their seat and actually do something.*

The man handed the flyer back to her and said, "I don't see any way that dog belongs to anyone. Just purely an orphan."

She was pretty well convinced now that there was no way to find Wiley's owner. But just to complete her effort, she taped up the flyers on a handful of trees and telephone poles in the area, and then drove into the woods to continue with her plans to meet with Romy deVere and explore her astonishing past. And when they drove past the place in the woods where she'd found Wiley in the middle of the night—could it really have been not even two weeks ago?—she looked over at him. He had his head down, and his tail had curled tightly between his hind legs. She reached a hand to him and stroked the soft Mohawk of hair on his head, then stroked down his back to comfort him. She could feel the quiver that ran through his whole body, and she was sure he knew where he was, and remembered—or certainly felt—the terror and abandonment of that night when he'd been put out, alone and helpless, probably to die, by people who should have known better.

Maybe, she thought, if they'd found a beautiful dog, a dog they could have shown off to their friends and relatives back in Moline, a dog everyone would have admired, then maybe they'd have been eager to keep him and thought themselves lucky to have acquired something valuable instead of an ugly liability.

"But the little boy wanted you, Wiley. The little boy knew your value. And I bet that little boy will grow up to be a better man than his father!"

It was a rebellious thought, but it made Gena feel good. And by the time they were driving into the clearing in front of Romy deVere's cabin, Wiley was alert and happy

Chapter Nineteen

The photo crew's van was already there, and they were setting up their equipment inside the cabin. The front door was open and they were in and out, getting light and speed settings, measuring distances, adjusting for the sun and the shadows. In the little bedroom at the back, Nell and the hairdressers were tending to Romy's makeup and hair, getting her ready to be photographed.

"So many years it's been," Romy said, with a wave of greeting to Gena as she came into the room. "I thought I was finished with this. This fussing with my face—don't they realize—'Let her paint an inch thick,' Hamlet said, and he was right, 'to this favor she must come.'" She paused, gazing into the mirror for a long minute, as though she was remembering how it was so long ago, when this was her life every day, makeup artists preparing her for the camera. "Well. Shakespeare is always right. All the paint in the world won't keep you from the grave."

"Ms. deVere," Nell said, dusting a thick makeup brush across those famous cheekbones, "you have an exquisite face. I don't care if it was sixty years ago or today, you are an incredibly beautiful woman. What's more, you know the old saying: 'At fifty, every woman has the face she deserves.' And it's true. I've made up some of the most famous women in America, and I can tell you must have lived a good life, because yours is still the face of a great beauty."

Romy laughed. "Then why all this fuss?"

"Because," Gena said as she put down her bag and took a seat in a spot out of the way, "you are making some wonderful art, and it is as though a whole new and remarkable life has begun in a life that was already full and fulfilling."

"And what I'm doing," Nell said, "is just for the camera. For light balance, and to emphasize bone structure and all of that. The camera seems to love looking at you, and we want to help it do just that. But you don't need me to tell you about it. You've been hearing it from makeup people for years, haven't you?"

"I've been hearing it from more than makeup people. I don't mind. It's like the great athletes. They too, must bear the adulation of great masses of the public. They must hear and read constantly about their remarkable feats, the records they've broken, those records that are being threatened by newcomers—and the multimillion-dollar contracts their agents have won for them. I was luckier, in some ways. An athlete, no matter how great, comes to the time when the body won't perform anymore. As an actress, I was able to perform somewhat longer, past the years of my freshest beauty. I was able to get roles, even a couple of very good roles, well into my sixties, as long as I was willing to play older parts. I didn't mind. I am an actress, after all, and the character is the challenge, not the cheekbones."

Romy probably didn't notice that Gena had discreetly slipped her phone from her bag and was recording her comments. *"The character is the challenge, not the cheekbones." Good one. Might be the title of the piece.*

"But Gena," Romy was talking to Gena's reflection in the mirror. "You didn't tell me you were bringing a visitor to our meeting today." With a gesture, she indicated Wiley, who was posed elegantly across Gena's lap. "I have Qualtinger locked up in his dog run out back today, to keep him out of everyone's way. Can you imagine the havoc he would create, like a big bear getting into everything, toppling the equipment, chewing up the cables? But look at the little imp you've brought. What fun. Bring him here—him? her?—please, introduce me."

"This is Wiley. He's a he. I think I should hold him. I haven't had him more than a few days, and I'm not sure how friendly he is."

"Nonsense!" Romy took him right from Gena's hands with an imperiousness born of decades of stardom. "Dogs and I always get along very well."

And indeed, Wiley seemed totally comfortable in Romy's hands and was already trying to lick her face, which, since it had just been so carefully made up, she held away from him, laughing. "No, no, Wiley. I can't allow you to spoil the beautiful mask that has been made of my face by this clever woman." She smiled at Nell. "Tell me, Ms. Magano. Do you know this breed? Not many people do."

Nell looked Wiley over, took in the funny Mohawk on his head, his hairless body, his fragile-looking legs, and said, "I've never seen anything like him before."

"This, Ms. Magano, is a much maligned breed. Isn't that right, Gena?" Gena smiled at her in the mirror.

"The amazing thing is, I found Wiley that day I was driving back to New York after you and I met for the first interview about your work. Do you remember? It was raining very hard that day." And she described the phantom flat tire and the almost-magical discovery of a drenched and whimpering dog. "So I took him home with me. My boyfriend wasn't happy about it, but I decided to keep him, anyway."

"Because you fell in love with him, no? I see it in your eyes. But how could you not? He is a very sweet dog. And a beautiful one, too. He is also a very lucky dog—that you stopped just then. Just when he must have thought all was lost." She turned away from the mirror and looked directly at Gena. "Do you believe in fate, my dear? In kismet?"

Gena was silent, a little embarrassed by the question.

"I made a movie once," Romy said, "long ago, before I left Europe. It was called *Kismet*. It was a silly movie. And quite scandalous, because I played an odalisque—you know, a concubine in a Turkish harem—and I allowed myself to appear naked. What did I care? I was seventeen and I knew I was beautiful. I *wanted* the world to look at me. And because the world did look at me, it was that movie—my kismet—that made me famous, and made it possible for me to escape Europe in a very dangerous time. I came to America, my husband and my father and I. And I became wonderfully successful. So," she looked into Wiley's face as she held him before her, "we must believe in kismet, no?" She smiled at him, as though they understood each other very well, and then turned him so that they looked into the mirror together. "Is it not the truth, my dear?"

And Gena thought she could not possibly argue with this woman who had made such an extraordinary success of her life, so she said only, "It was certainly true for you, and for Wiley. And maybe for me, too, because I feel lucky that I have him. Though he's causing plenty of trouble between me and my boyfriend."

"Oh?" Both Romy and Nell turned to look at her. Nell's face plainly said, *I want to hear about this.* But Romy was even more direct. "You must tell me all about it. I have a passion for girlish gossip." Gena was surprised to realize she was not offended. She waved off Nell with a laugh and a shake of her head that said, *No way, not going down that road.* Gena was smart enough to know that sharing secrets with colleagues was a sure career-ender. But about Romy, she was not so sure. Perhaps later on, when they were alone.

In any case, the talk about dogs and beauty and men needed to stop, because Romy's hair was done, her makeup was perfect, and the photo people were ready to shoot. Gena and Nell moved out of the way and Ira and his crew went to work.

It was a pleasure to watch Romy deVere respond to the cameras. She knew all about camera angles and lighting and her own best presentation. She knew how to make the most of the opportunity to show off the paintings she'd been producing. She led them through a tour of her studio, which was a section of the cabin that had been built to her very deliberate specifications as to space and light sources. And she'd agreed to a second day of shooting at the gallery in Shanesville devoted to the work of local artists. The photo people were happy to be working with a skilled subject—and they were loving the chance to add to the decades-long catalog of photographic studies of this beautiful woman—once a raven-haired, sultry icon and now a wise, lively, humorous woman of ninety-seven years.

Gena and Nell had stationed themselves near the doorway, where they could watch all the activity but also step quickly outside if the camera people needed them out of the way. And while they waited and watched, Nell leaned her head close to Gena's and said, "Gena, sweetie, you know I love you dearly. But I don't care what the famous and gorgeous Romy deVere says: That's one helluva funny looking dog you have there. I'm sure he's the sweetest thing and you love him like a brother, but that animal looks like a cartoon of a dog."

Gena was getting used to this line of quasi-comedy, and she was beginning to be tired of it. Her protective spirit was roused—she couldn't let people poke fun at Wiley, but she also couldn't afford to get mad at everyone who did, especially people she really liked, people she worked with, people who thought they were just being cute and friendly. She was going to have to think up a good comeback that kept a light touch while still closing off the teasing.

But while she was thinking about it, Ira Garlen was passing them in the doorway, moving his crew outside, where views of Romy's cabin and the surrounding woods were to be a part of the story. Ira paused, looked at Wiley and then at Gena.

"Is he yours, Gena? Or does he belong to Romy?"

"His name is Wiley and he's mine, and are you going to tell me how weird he is, too?"

"Weird? Not at all. I know this breed. I know what people say about them, but they don't deserve it. They're very elegant dogs." He took a step back, and for a long minute he studied Wiley with a professionally appraising eye, and then he made a decision. "I heard you guys talking about the dog—and I heard what Ms. deVere said about him. And I'm thinking I might have an idea that would work nicely for this story. With the right lighting, posing him carefully, we could get some shots of the two of them together that would really add to the drama of this piece. What do you think, Gena? Would you be willing to let me use him?"

"Are you kidding? An Ira Garlen photo of my Wiley? In a *Lady Fair* story with Romy deVere?"

"We'll pay you scale for him. I have a stack of releases in the van."

"Omigod!" She picked Wiley up and held him close, face to face. "Wiley! You're about to become a professional model. And with a great beauty. Lucky you!" And to Ira, she said, "What are you thinking of doing with him?"

"I want to pose him like that ancient Egyptian god. Face to face with Ms. deVere."

"Beauty and the beast?" Nell suggested. Her sarcasm reminded Gena of schoolyard teasing. She was liking Nell less at this moment.

"Not at all," Ira said, brushing away Nell's teasing. "What I have in mind is a classic photograph of two powerful mythic figures sharing their moment together. I am thinking of Anubis, one of the gods of ancient Egypt. Wiley has the same has long, pointy ears and pointy snout as Anubis. The god sits very erect, looking straight ahead, very formal and secure. He knows he commands the end of each person's life. You know the one, don't you? You've seen the figure."

"No, Ira. Sorry. I have no idea who you're talking about," Gena said. She turned to Nell. "Nell? Do you know what Ira's talking about?"

"Not me, either." Nell looked blank

"Oh, you young people." Ira was laughing. "Don't they teach anything in the schools anymore? History? Art? Ancient religions?"

"I took a graphic arts class once," Nell said, a little cowed by Ira's scolding.

"Well, go to the Met. In the gift shop, they sell a little black statuette that looks like what I have in mind. The god Anubis. Wiley's a dead ringer for him." Abruptly, Ira looked at his watch. "I've got to move on with this next location. Gena, if you're okay with my idea, one of the guys can get you the release form out of the van."

"Oh, I'm okay with it. For sure." And to Wiley, she said, "Wiley, my dear, your picture is going to be in *Lady Fair* magazine. Do you know how many models would kill for this chance?"

Wiley said nothing of course, but he licked Gena's face while Nell looked away disdainfully.

Romy loved the idea and was full of suggestions for illustrating Ira's concept of god and goddess. There was much fussing with hair and camera angles and light adjustments and posing this way and that, with Wiley being incredibly agreeable and cooperative. Turned out he was a natural ham and plainly got quickly into the whole project. But Gena suffered torments very much like those every mother knows, watching her child perform for an audience, for a camera, for a judge. She glowed with pride and was at the same time desperate to interfere, to make her dog's every move a better one, a perfect one, a more interesting one. Fortunately, she was also sane enough to leave the professionals to their work, and forced herself to suffer in silence. Therefore, all went swimmingly, and after a half hour of poses and light adjustments, and having the rare treat of watching Romy deVere slip instantly and seamlessly into her old role of actress and star, the session was done.

It was evening by the time Ira was ready to pack up. He said he was starving and would take his whole crew into town and find a bar or a restaurant, or at least a pizza joint. Nell and Gena were invited to come along, and Nell was eager to join them, but Gena had some more work to do with Romy.

"You go ahead," she said. "I need to tie up some loose ends with Romy, and she's invited me to stay on and share some homemade goulash with her. I won't starve. And I'll catch up with you guys tomorrow." As they all drove away into the woods, headed for Shanesville, she called after them, "Drive safely."

With Wiley in her arms, she waved goodbye. And then, feeling she'd at last come to the real purpose of this day, she turned back into the cabin and prepared to see if Romy was willing to open some of the secret doors to her life.

Chapter Twenty

"Come," Romy said. In the kitchen, she was taking a pot of Hungarian goulash from the oven, where she had been keeping it at a low simmer for hours. She called to Gena to join her. "Come." The small table was already set, and she motioned to a chair at one side. "Sit. Be comfortable. I have made for us a goulash like our cook in Vienna used to prepare." She ladled the stew into the bowls at their places. "When I am in a nostalgic mood, I always need to prepare Frau Leinberger's goulash. My God, could that woman cook! Such things she taught me. Hungarian *goulas* and *apfelstrudel*. And her *vanillekipferl*! Those little crescents made of ground walnuts. Rolled in powdered vanilla sugar. She could make a hundred of them, and each one would be identical in shape and size, like they were made by a machine. And *Dobos torte, Malakoff torte, Germknödl*. I weep just to remember." She sat and placed her napkin neatly in her lap. "But I think we have much to talk about, you and I, and this goulash reminds me of long ago. At my age, the well of memory is very deep, and some things have been covered over, meant to be forgotten."

"But there is something that is trying to come up to the surface, isn't there, Romy?" Gena caught herself. "I'm sorry. I mean Ms. deVere. That just slipped out."

"No. Of course. We shall be *per du*, as they say in Austria. 'Familiar.' First names. As though I care about the formalities. Since I was a girl, I have never been formal. America was a blessing for me in so many ways. The informality was wonderful." Romy broke off a small hunk of bread, slogged it around in the goulash gravy, and gobbled it up neatly. "And you are right, of course. There are secrets, and there is one secret in particular I am hoping to open up to the world."

"And you thought I would catch on, somehow, that there was something in your history that was worth digging up. But I had to figure it out without being told that the 'something' existed. And whatever it was, it was hidden somewhere in our conversation. You were hiding it in plain sight, weren't you?"

"You have a sharp ear. And a perceptive eye. I'd sensed that about you. I told you nothing I haven't told others. But you were different: you listened." Romy scooped up some more gravy on a bit of bread. She ate it, dabbed at her mouth with her napkin, and sat back in her chair. "So tell me, Gena. What did you hear when you listened to me?"

"At first I heard only the same story of your life that you've told other interviewers. But I caught a special vibe when you told me your real name. Before you became Romy deVere, you were Lotte Elisabeth Kanfer."

The tiniest smile appeared at the corner of Romy's mouth.

"And then you spoke of your father, Thomas Kanfer. You said he was a brilliant engineer—and that he shared so much of his work and his thinking with you. And then, Romy, you sat back in your chair, as you are doing now. And there was something...a kind of challenge, but a challenge buried in a disappointment...I don't know how to describe it, but whatever it was, it told me to pay attention. And then you said, 'I could almost, if I wished, make my living as an electrical engineer.'"

Romy took a great, deep breath. The kind of deep breath that eases tension—and braces for what's coming.

Gena spoke simply and she spoke quietly: "I found the patent applications, Romy." There was the tiniest quiver at the corner of Romy's mouth. "At first, the subject meant nothing to me. I had to do a bit of self-educating to understand that your father had developed a system that would allow the delivery of torpedoes and bombs by remote control. It was invaluable technology in wartime, and many decades ahead of its time."

Romy's chest was heaving but she continued to sit quietly.

"I found, also, that there was a whole series of patent applications following that first one. And not all of them were filed by your father, were they, Romy?"

Romy remained silent, but it seemed to Gena she could actually hear Romy's heart beating.

"Some of them," Gena continued, "were filed by Liesl Hardtmann." Romy nodded ever so slightly, as though afraid to acknowledge that Gena was on the right track. "Liesl is, of course, a nickname for Elisabeth. And, fortunately, I had already read enough of your biography to recognize the name Hardtmann—the name of your first husband, Hans Hardtmann, the man you'd married when you were only seventeen, the producer of your first film, *Kismet*."

There was a long silence—at least one full minute as the second hand went round the clock. Romy was breathing hard.

"How did you know to look for those patents?" she finally asked.

"I didn't. But I knew to follow Tommy Kanfer's trail. There was something about the way you spoke of him that told me he was the key to the secret you were so carefully *not* telling me. There wasn't much on him, actually. But one obscure citation led me to the US Patent Office. And then, when I saw the subject of that first application, I remembered you saying that you could have made your living as an electrical engineer. And there, too, I'd felt some special message in the way you said it. From there, it was simple. Each door opened up the next, in turn."

By now, Romy was beaming at her. "You will understand," Romy said, "I have waited a long time for someone to bring all this to the surface." She got up from the table. "I can hardly breathe. This is a very special day for me." From the fridge, she took a bottle of Austrian white wine. "From the Burgenland," she said. "It seems appropriate to the occasion."

"But, Romy, I don't understand. The real mystery is why you kept it a secret. And why do you want it to come out now?"

"I always wanted it to come out."

She poured the wine into their glasses.

Gena didn't have to ask the obvious question.

Romy said, "I'd been forced to sign a paper."

"Forced?"

"If I wanted to work. The studio was not willing that the public should know me in any way except as a scandalous, raven-haired, sultry femme fatale."

"But that's so crazy. You'd think they'd *want* to market you as an extraordinary woman, an incredibly beautiful and sexy woman who is also a brilliant scientist."

Romy's laugh was bitter. "Those were different times, Gena. Almost eighty years ago. In those days, women's roles were carefully manufactured to reflect prescribed images of what women were supposed to be. Hollywood insisted that any woman who was a brilliant scientist—as you so kindly put it—had to wear glasses and shapeless suits and mannish shoes. And her hair couldn't be raven. Only a dowdy, mousy brown would do. She certainly couldn't be a world-class beauty. The studio people thought the public couldn't accept anything other than a foolish stereotype. They believed that a different reality would scare them away from the box office.

They were convinced that the truth about me would have a bad effect on their profit margin. So their lawyers drew up a nondisclosure agreement that forced me to be absolutely silent about my scientific work. Forever."

She paused, took a sip of her wine, put the glass down, and looked away for a moment, and Gena sensed that she was about to reveal something more. Romy apparently needed some time before she decided to go on, and Gena wisely stayed silent.

Finally, with a deep sigh, and still looking away from Gena, as though she was confessing something shameful, Romy said, "The truth is, at that time, I really didn't care if my scientific work was kept hidden. I was young and eager for fame, and much more interested in being that raven-haired, sultry, scandalous, femme fatale, with Hollywood recognition and a successful acting career ahead of me. I was ambitious and self-centered and valued movie stardom far above scientific achievement."

"But now you want recognition for that, too?"

Romy nodded.

"What changed?"

Romy sighed again. "Many things, I suppose. Women have changed. We are growing up. All over the world, women are beginning to run their own lives, wherever they can. And the times have changed. It is almost eighty years from then to now. The inevitable growth of experience, wisdom, patience. One takes inventory of one's life as the end comes close. One realizes that some things have lasting importance and others don't. My name is virtually unknown today—go out on the street in any city in America and ask, 'Who is Romy deVere?' and only very old people may remember the name. And no one sees my films anymore—except perhaps film buffs, students of film, teachers, scholars who write about the old days. The scandals that lit up the tabloid world in those days were little more than children's innocent fairy tales compared to what screams at readers today."

And now Romy leaned forward, as though her reflective mood had shifted to one of serious engagement.

"Gena," she said, "I remember the work my father and I did all those years ago, together in his study—working out the details of what we called a 'radio steering device,' figuring out carrier waves of shifting frequencies, working to find a technology that would keep bombardiers and battleships safer. And now I see the peacetime fruit of that work all around me. I see it in the cell phone you are using, and in the computers and laptops, and all the other electronic devices on which the explosion of instantaneous worldwide communication depend. I see it in the massive use of social media and all its political and economic consequences. Today's Wi-Fi and Bluetooth, the cloud interface, the GPS in your car—Gena, it all, *all*, rests on the work Thomas Kanfer and his eager daughter did, sitting there in his study. We were so engaged—oh, I can remember as though it was yesterday, we were so fascinated by the possibilities. We understood the enormous military value our work would have. We understood the contribution we were making to the war effort of our new country and its allies." She was glowing with the thrill of the memories that she was sharing, memories she'd been forbidden to share for so many years. Her beautiful deep blue eyes were flashing and her hands were clasped tightly, as though to keep her excitement from bursting out of her. "But we had absolutely no awareness then of what the world's population would be holding in its hand decades later. Because of us! Do you understand, Gena? *Because of us!*"

In her mind, Gena's story for *Lady Fair* was practically writing itself. *Oh, Lord. This is going to be so great!*

"And now," Gena said, "you want to come out from behind the curtain, to come out of the shadows. You want it to be no longer hidden. You want the role that you, Romy deVere, played in this century's great electronic development to be seen and recognized by its proper audience. You want your work—and your father's work—to be acknowledged by the entire world. You want to be known as the full person you are and have been, and not only as a Hollywood stereotype."

"Exactly. I realize that I am still ambitious, though I live quietly here in my little cabin in the woods. I know now that I still want the world to know me, and not because I was once beautiful. I want the world to know me because I did something important. My father and I did something important, and I am so proud of it, Gena. I want to stand up and take the credit for what we did. Perhaps my father would not have cared. But I do. And I want to be able to speak about our work, without being gagged by that piece of paper I signed."

"And the only legally safe way that could happen," Gena said, "was for someone else to come along and spill the beans without your having said a word."

"You have understood it exactly."

The two women were silent, each thoughtful in her own appreciation of the other. Then each, slowly, began to smile, knowing that something good had happened here. And gradually, each woman felt her own small smile grow into a broad grin, broader and broader, until both women simultaneously broke out into uproarious and totally uncontrollable laughter, the infectious laughter that feeds on itself and cannot end until it reaches exhaustion. On Romy's part, it was the inevitable result of decades of needing to keep a complex secret under tight control. And for Gena, it was a recognition that she'd engaged in an almost silly bit of mischief, that she was guilty of an impish complicity in a vaguely illicit scheme. As though she'd been a willing co-conspirator, helping Romy outfox the wicked Hollywood fat cats.

And so the two women drank more wine, let the dogs out to play, reviewed some of the details Gena would need for the magazine article, and then decided that Gena had had too much wine to drive back to New York that night, so she bedded down on the sofa in the front room, with her phone alarm set for six so she could get back to the office by nine, and with Wiley curled up next to her, she slept the—almost—dreamless sleep that comes after a day of good work done and the prospect of good work to be done again tomorrow.

There was one dream, though... It started out scary, with Warren playing golf, trying hard to drive the ball at Wiley, who was running frantically this way and that across the greens, with Warren's boss standing by and laughing and cheering Warren on. And then Gena ran out onto the green to save Wiley, and Warren was driving the balls at her, too, but she grabbed Wiley up and ran away to the dog park behind the Met, making sure it was before nine in the morning, which was the safe time for dogs.

Chapter Twenty-one

"Where the hell have you been?" Warren was not at his best early in the morning.

"I'm on my way home. I told you where I was going."

"Not a word from you all night, and all I know is you're up in Connecticut somewhere with that old movie person. At least you could have called."

"I told you last time: There's no cell phone connection up there in the woods. I had to wait till I got to the highway."

Why did he always make her feel like a little girl, explaining why she forgot her homework or lost her mittens?

"And I'm supposed to wait around until you feel like remembering about me? I didn't know you were going to stay overnight."

"I'm on the freeway, Warren. Can't talk and drive. Talk to you later." She shut off the call and tossed the phone into her bag.

Not worth driving dangerously just to listen to him scold me.

I wonder what Romy would have done.

That was a new thought. What *would* Romy have done? The answer was hovering somewhere beneath her conscious thought. But she wasn't ready for it yet.

Instead, she engaged Wiley in her ruminations. He was, after all, a perfectly nonconfrontational listener. He didn't argue with her, he didn't catch her up in self-serving defenses, he was happy sticking his nose out the bit of window she'd cracked open, and he never got bored or demanded to know, "Are we there yet?" Every now and then he dropped down from his stance, front paws up on the edge of the door, and turned to Gena as though to assure her he was still listening to her. Then, after a nuzzle against her arm, he'd go back to letting the wind blow against his nose and ruffle the bit of hair on the tips of his ears.

"I don't know what he's so mad about. It's not like he's never away on business, and if he is, I always know he may be kept away longer than expected." Almost a whole mile of freeway passed beneath her wheels before she spoke again. "And he knew I was going to be out of cell phone range." After another mile: "Like whatever I was doing, I should be thinking about him."

That's when Wiley came over and put a paw on her arm, and she looked away from the road just long enough to nod an acknowledgement of his attention. "Here I am," she said, her eyes back on the road, "with the biggest story I've ever had, practically dropped into my lap, and I'm sorry, Warren"—now she addressed the imagined boyfriend—"I can't help it if you were not being attended to while I was putting together a real scoop, one that will have people talking, and, what's more, a story that wouldn't have happened at all if I hadn't done some pretty clever journalistic sleuthing." She realized she was pouting like a little girl. "I think you should be proud of me." But her imaginary Warren just scowled his disapproval at her, and her one-sided conversation had not resolved anything. Wiley went back to his scenery-watching and wind-sniffing and Gena turned on the radio and forced herself to stop thinking about Warren.

Anyway, her stomach was reminding her that she'd left Romy's cabin without stopping for breakfast, insisting she wasn't hungry, didn't have time, would get something along the way. Her real reason for leaving without a pause to eat had been that she wanted to get to the freeway, where she'd be able to call Warren as quickly as possible, but for some reason she didn't want to say that to Romy. But now that she'd had her brief call with Warren and he would no longer need to be worrying about her, she decided to stop as soon as possible to get something to eat—and give Wiley a chance to pee. And with that decision, she found her mind focused on the day ahead, the story she'd be writing, the details that needed to be put together, the further research that might be needed. Already, the outline of the story was taking shape in her head.

Out loud, she said, "The character is the challenge, not the cheekbones."

These words would be the opening sentence.

* * * *

Even with a quick stop at a service station for coffee and a couple of doughnuts, and giving Wiley a minute to visit a couple of trees at the edge

of the station's parking area, she was back on Seventy-Third Street before
eight-thirty. Warren had already left for the office, and when she came
into the apartment she found a note on the kitchen table:

> *Viv says she'll come by to walk the dog. She has the key.*
>
> *Try to make some regular arrangement for him, okay?*
>
> *I don't like people coming in here when no one's home.*

There was a second note, next to the first.

> *Do we really need to have a dog?*

Chapter Twenty-two

"Tell Marge I'm glad she's back, and I need to see her as soon as she has a minute. Maybe more than a minute. Important."

Gena was bursting with the news for Marge and sent Selma scurrying off with the message before she even got herself settled in. A scoop on *two* stories! The wedding of Sonny Gaile and Tim Fine on Monday, and the revelations about the secret wartime inventions of a long-ago beauty icon. They'd be reaching two markets—the younger readers with the Sonny Gaile story, and their more "mature" readers, the women who thought they knew all about Romy deVere but would now be astounded to learn from the pages of *Lady Fair* the secrets she'd kept hidden for more than seventy years.

She'd no sooner got her stuff unloaded when her phone signaled a message from Marge:

> *Good news? Bad news? Can it wait till noon?*
> *Swamped up here.*

She texted right back:

> *Good news. It can wait till noon. Welcome back.*

There was plenty for her to do till noon. She'd had no chance to talk with Ira about the new angle on the shoot in Tennessee, so she called his office to arrange to meet with him at ten. Brittney had already faxed over the nondisclosure forms that everyone would have to sign. As soon as the legal department okayed the forms and got them signed, they'd be faxed back to Brittney.

Ira took the shift in the assignment with no fuss. That was one of the great things about working with him. Never any dramatics, just purely professional. But he loved the idea of a wedding at Sonny's cabin and got Brittney's contact information from Gena so he could talk with her about the physical layout—indoors? outdoors?—time of day for the ceremony, sunlight orientation, what people would be wearing. Before Gena left his office, he stopped her on her way out to say that it had been a big moment in his life to have had a chance to photograph the great Romy deVere, and that he looked forward to the story.

"Oh, it's going to be an interesting one," Gena said. "And your photos are always great, Ira. I know Romy's going to love them."

She left him with a big smile and a thumbs-up.

Barely back at her desk and her phone was ringing. Warren was calling.

"Did you remember to pick up another bottle of Glenlivet? We're practically out and I told you last week—"

She cut him off. "Can't talk now, Warren. Super busy. I'll try to remember on my way home tonight."

And as she hung up, she heard him saying, "How could you manage to forget? I specifically—"

She sat still for a moment, feeling set back on her heels. She'd been feeling so pleased with herself, so energetic and eager about all the positive things that were happening. But in Warren's eyes, she'd failed again. Because she'd forgotten a chore he'd assigned to her.

She clamped her lips together and said aloud, "Nuts to you, Warren!"

She was about to turn her attention to the deVere story and the materials she'd want to show Marge, but again she was interrupted. This time it was a call from Viv.

"Just thought you'd like to know: I went over to your place to take Wiley out. And we were walking along Madison, right by that store where they sell the flowers, on the corner at Seventy-Ninth Street? Next to the real estate place?"

"I know the place."

"Well, we were walking along there and a man stopped me. He said, 'Do I recognize Wiley?' So I figured he must know you."

"Did he have a small white dog with him?"

"Yes, he did. You know who he is?"

"Yes. And you do, too. Or, at least you know the dog. That's Sweetie Pie. Remember her? Harriet van Siclen's Powderpuff Crested? And the man is Mrs. Van Siclen's brother, Paul. He's taking care of her dog while she's in Australia." She paused. She knew Viv was going to be full of questions. "We've met a couple of times, dog walking."

"He's good-looking, in a hedge-fund manager sort of way. You know. Sedate and ruthless."

"I didn't think he was ruthless."

"Maybe I'm wrong."

"Hmm."

"But he's kind of cute."

"Kind of."

"How old, do you think?"

"I don't know. Late thirties, maybe."

"Forty?"

"I don't think so."

Both women were silent for a moment.

"Anyway," Viv said, finally, "he asked for you. Said he hadn't seen you for a couple of days. I told him you'd been away. I didn't tell him you were already back in New York."

"No reason why you should."

Another long pause.

"So. That's it?"

"Of course. Why?"

"I don't know, Gena. I just thought he looked sort of nice."

"Come on, Viv. Are you trying to promote something between Paul and me?"

"I'm just saying."

"I know how you feel about Warren."

"I'm just saying."

"Well, you'll have to stop 'just saying.' You're going to have to let it go, Viv. Anyway, I gotta go. Meeting with Marge Webster at noon."

"All right. But the guy is kind of cute."

"Good*bye,* Viv!"

"Okay, okay."

* * * *

"Okay, Gena, what have you got for me?"

You'd never know, looking at Marge Webster sitting there at her desk, in her cool Chanel suit and her picture-perfect dark hair and her great jewelry, all gold and a mile thick, that she'd just come in on a redeye flight from Milan after a week in the hectic and highly concentrated rush of a major fashion event.

"So glad you're back," Gena said. "A lot going on here. First of all, there's a big, *big* addition to the Sonny Gaile story." Marge lifted her head and pursed her lips, all attention. "Sonny's publicist called. Brittney Brisken. You know Sonny and his partner, Tim Fine, have been together for over a year?" Marge nodded. That was one story that was familiar to anyone who stayed clued in to celebrity news. "Well, item number one: Sonny and Tim are getting married." Marge's eyebrows rose. This *was* news. She could smell what was coming. "And they're giving *Lady Fair* an exclusive on the story." Marge added a nod of her head to the pursing of her lips.

"Go on."

"You'd already left, and we didn't want to trust any kind of communication about it, not by mail or phone or fax or text or email, not carrier pigeon or smoke signal. They want absolute secrecy until publication. The camera crew, Nell and her people, et cetera, et cetera. No one. The nondisclosure paperwork is at legal now, and if they approve and everything is signed by everyone here, everything should be ready by Monday, which is the day we were scheduled to go down there anyway for the shoot."

Marge's wheels were already rolling. "If we really push," she said, "we might be able to have the story ready for the next issue. We should try to do that. No way this wedding is going to stay a secret much longer than that. Stories like this are so porous. Can't keep it from leaking all over the place. Even though we know our people will be reliable, you can bet there'll be someone else ready to sell it to the tabloids. Or at least it will be on social media in no time. But they've given us an exclusive, so we need to make the most of it, if we can. I'll have to pull something to make room for it. Would you say two thousand words, plus photos?"

"Whatever you say, Marge. Two thousand should be good."

"I'll meet with layout, have them clear the space. And I'm counting on you to deliver the copy."

"Of course."

"But Gena. Why you? No offense, sweetie, but you're young and fairly new. Why did they hand this story over to us here at *Lady Fair*? What magic spell did you throw over them when you were down there in Tennessee?"

"I have no idea. I was surprised, too."

"Well then, I'm just happy to count our blessings and move on. What's next? Where are you on the Romy deVere story?"

"Ah. That one is even more interesting."

Marge's eyebrows rose again. "This I want to hear."

Gena had all the deVere material in a Redweld expanding file. She took out the papers, put them in front of Marge, and, with careful explanations along the way, laid the whole story out. Marge listened intently. And silently. She went carefully through the patent office documents and the other papers, the scientific articles and the newspaper articles.

"This is a totally different kind of story," Marge said. "Much more meat here. You have a major piece here."

"That's what I was thinking, too, Marge. This goes to the heart of stereotypes about beauty, about beautiful women. It touches on the generational changes, the politics and the economics of the movie industry, the choices they made, their influence on the role—the roles—of women, then and now. I'm really eager to sink my teeth into this one. If you're okay with it, I'd like a little more time to do this one."

"Do you have a timetable in mind?"

"Not yet. I just got back this morning. But I can have something for you by tomorrow. Will that be okay?"

"Tomorrow morning. First thing." She looked at a photo of Romy that accompanied one of the articles. "My God, she sure was a beauty."

"She still is. And Ira was really happy with the shots he was getting. He had some interesting ideas—but you'll see. We'll put something together to show you."

Marge studied Gena as though she was seeing her in a totally new way. Getting to know this new person who'd emerged out of the young, raw writer who'd been only a new intern not so long ago.

Finally, she spoke. "I'm impressed. This is good work, Gena."

Gena tried to take this with professionally cool aplomb. But praise from the editor in chief was not handed out liberally, and she felt enormously honored.

"Thank you, Marge. That means a lot to me."

"All good." Marge was already moving on to the next matter before her. "Now get to work. And close the door. I have calls to make."

And with a wave of Marge's hand, Gena was dismissed.

* * * *

Outside of Marge's office, once she'd closed the door, Gena walked a little way down the hall, then stopped, made sure no one was around, and allowed herself one terrific, celebratory fist pump.

"Yes!" she whispered.

She'd hit a home run. Wow!

"I am so proud!"

Then she scooted back to her office. There was plenty to do now. She couldn't wait to get home that night, to tell Warren all about it. This was the kind of success that would impress Warren.

But there was still one more interruption in her day: Selma stopped her in the hall.

"While you were in Marge's office, some man called. Paul something, started with a B, but I didn't get it. Number's on your desk. He sounded like you know him."

And Selma disappeared around the corner.

Gena put all her stuff on the desk and then sat herself down, surprised, for she felt nervous about calling Paul. She needed to think for a moment: what was she to say? Like a schoolgirl. She cleared her throat, felt silly, and then dialed his number. When he answered, he said, "Hello, Gena," and his voice had a smile in it.

"Hello, Paul. Sorry I missed your call. I was in a meeting. But this is a nice surprise."

"I won't keep you," he said. "I just wanted to tell you, when I took the Pie to her day care place this morning, I talked to them about their 'sibling' policy. That's what they call it. They have a discounted rate if you have more than one dog staying with them, so I got them to agree to take Wiley as Sweetie Pie's sibling. As a favor to me. They kind of owe me. I've done some legal work for them, so they were willing to bend the rules a little bit—and they'll bill it to my account. My firm's account, actually." He could hear her objection forming and he headed her off. "And before you start protesting, let me just say it would make me happy if you'll let me do this for you. I hate to think of your having to navigate through your boyfriend's opposition, and it will keep the stress level down if there's a safe place for Wiley to stay every day."

There was silence—until Paul said, "Gena?"

"I don't know what to say."

"'Thank you' would be nice." He was laughing.

Gena laughed, too. "Of course, thank you. It's just that I'm stunned."

"Well, listen. I called your office because I didn't have your phone number. If you'll give it to me, I'll text Dog Prep's contact information to you. They're expecting to hear from you, and they'll tell you what they need. You know, Wiley's shot records, medical history, et cetera. And you can take him over there in the morning."

"I still don't know what to say. Besides 'thank you,' again. This is very kind. And generous."

"My pleasure. And maybe we'll meet sometime. At Dog Prep. With our dogs."

"I'd like that," Gena said. And she meant it. She was probably not aware of the very nice smile on her face, and she was certainly not aware of the very nice smile that was on Paul Brackman's face, too.

Chapter Twenty-three

"Did you remember the Glenlivet?" Warren looked up from his laptop as she came through the door.

Surprised and instantly on the defensive, not even entirely into the apartment yet, Gena was stopped in her tracks. Wiley came running to her and she picked him up and held him in front of her chest, as though he'd be a shield against Warren's apparent irritation.

"No. I didn't pick up the Glenlivet. I had too much to think about—"

"Honestly, Gena." Warren interrupted her. "Was it so much to ask? It's not like you're saving the world, or busy doing rocket science. The least you could do is remember a little request like stopping at the liquor store on your way home. Like it's so far out of your way."

She put down her things on the nearest chair. "I've been away since yesterday morning, and I've got some really big stories going on, and I just didn't think of your liquor needs. And you know what else? I'm tired. I've been seriously busy, and I don't see why you couldn't pick up the Glenlivet yourself if it's so important to you."

"Oh, that's just fine. Like I've got nothing to do all day except run household errands. Maybe I was busy doing something a little more important, like managing multimillion-dollar transactions. And what kind of big stories are you doing? Is Madame Fifi going to be wearing shorter skirts this year? Or are they going to be longer? Or maybe longer in the back and shorter in the front? Like, who cares?"

"You're right, Warren. Nothing I'm doing is that important. I'm not making millions of dollars from it, so it certainly isn't anything you'd be interested in." She picked up Wiley's leash and snapped it onto his collar. "So why don't you just order us in some Chinese food while I take Wiley out, and after we have dinner, we can fight about your Scotch some more, and then about whose work is more important."

And then Gena did something she'd never done before: on the way out, she slammed the door behind her.

But Gena was incapable of being angry for very long. It just wasn't in her nature. After a twenty-minute walk around the neighborhood, she'd talked herself down from her flare-up and convinced herself that, after all, Warren had asked her a couple of times to take care of that little errand, and, after all, he did have important matters demanding his attention, and, after all, getting mad is so unattractive—and, after all, Warren did bring a lot more money into the household than she did, and if, perhaps, someday they did decide to get married and maybe even have children, wouldn't they likely have to rely more on his earnings than on hers? And so didn't it matter more that his time be devoted to his work, and so shouldn't the trivia of everyday life fall more on her shoulders than on his?

By the time she'd finished making all these excuses, she'd calmed herself down and was ready to go home and make up. And apologize for slamming that door. So perhaps it was fate—kismet?—that she came to this conclusion just as she was passing the local wine and liquor store on Third Avenue. Wiley was sniffing at the bricks below the store's front window, and the display of stock just happened to be a variety of whiskeys.

She laughed at the coincidence, and as she walked inside she said to Wiley, "Let's go make Warren happy."

She bought a bottle of Glenlivet and got the sales clerk to give her a bit of bright red ribbon to tie around the bottle's neck. "A peace offering," she explained to Wiley. "See?" She showed him the pretty bow she'd made. Wiley was unimpressed.

They rode up in the elevator with the young man who was delivering their dinner. She stopped him outside the apartment door, said she'd pay for the food right then, tipped him, waited for him to get into the elevator and disappear, and then let herself into the apartment.

"I'm home," she announced, "and I'm bringing dinner and a gift."

Warren was on the sofa in the living room with his laptop open on the coffee table, obviously busy with something work-related. He looked up at her, preoccupied.

"A gift?"

She put the brown paper bag of Chinese food down on the coffee table, next to his laptop, and handed him the bottle of Glenlivet.

"A peace offering," she said. "I'm sorry I got mad. I hate it when we fight. Let's not fight, okay, Warren?"

"We're not fighting, honey." He looked at the bottle, noticed the ribbon, smiled and put the bottle down next to the bag. "I just don't like it when you don't pay attention to me. Or to what I ask you to do. I just can't be bothered with the small stuff, and I rely on you to take care of those things for me." He got up from the sofa, came over to her, and put his arms around her. Wiley started to circle around them, yipping nervously. "And you're so good at taking care of the small stuff. I couldn't manage without you." He looked down at Wiley as though he'd like to kick him.

"But sometimes it's hard for me, too—having to take care of the small stuff. You're not the only one who has work to do. I have work to do, too. Maybe it's not so important, but it is my work and I can't just set it aside any old time you want me to pick up your dry cleaning or take something to the post office. Or"—she gestured toward the beribboned bottle of scotch on the coffee table—"go to the liquor store for you."

It was astonishing how suddenly Warren's mood changed. He stepped away from her abruptly, picked up the bottle, and took it to the bar. Wiley stayed close to Gena.

"Well." He managed to sound profoundly offended. "It's sure good to know how you really feel. Just in case I was thinking you liked being helpful. Helping me keep the decks clear so I can go out and bring home the big bucks. The bucks, by the way, that paid for most of the stuff we have here." He gestured around the room. "I thought I could count on you for support. Not for criticism."

"I support you, Warren."

"Yeah. Well, it doesn't sound like it." He clinked a couple of ice cubes from the ice bucket into a glass and poured a couple of fingers of scotch over them. "You know, there are plenty of girls would have been happy to be in your place. Prettier girls, too, I might add. It's not like you're the most gorgeous girl in the world."

Gena was stunned. They'd had arguments before, even a couple of snarling fights, but wow! He'd never been this mean.

"I can't believe you said what you just said."

Wiley started to bark.

"Well, look at you. You're skinny as a rail, not a curve anywhere on you, and could you maybe figure out how to do something a little more attractive with your hair or your makeup? You'd think you could have learned something from those glamour girls you work with."

"Warren, what's gotten into you? Why are you talking to me this way? I don't deserve this."

"Well, honey"—this time the endearment was sarcastic—"as long as you're choosing to be so honest about how you really feel, maybe you ought to hear what I'm thinking, too. Seems to me if you're going to go off on your high horse whenever you feel like it, anytime you get in a mood, then we need to rethink just what it is we actually do have here."

A hammer, it seemed, was hitting her in the stomach. And suddenly tears filled her eyes.

"What are you saying? Are you saying you want to end things between us?"

"Not at all. I'm just saying you're going to have to make some changes. I'm looking ahead, and I'm seeing my future, and I need you to fit in a little bit better. That's all."

Now the tears fell. She turned away to hide them.

Warren threw up a hand in exasperation. "Oh, that's just fine. Here come the waterworks."

And truly, the tears were now a flood. She picked up Wiley, who was barking excitedly, and without even stopping for her bag, her keys, or Wiley's leash, she ran out of the apartment.

"Gena!" Warren's shout echoed down the hallway as she rang for the elevator, but she didn't care, and she also didn't care when she heard their door slam shut on his muttered "God-*damn*!"

* * * *

She wandered around the neighborhood, feeling miserable and desolate for maybe fifteen minutes, but by then Wiley was getting heavy in her arms, and she couldn't let him off-leash on the city street. She couldn't bear the thought of going back to the apartment and dealing with Warren—not yet—so she checked her watch and saw that it was close to nine o'clock. She headed for the open dog area behind the museum.

It was a good choice. Wiley could stay close, which he seemed to want to do, but she could also be alone with her thoughts—and with this sudden upheaval in her life. It seemed too great to be kept in check, and now the tears were coming again, and because she'd come out without her bag or any money and she had no tissues or handkerchief with her, she could do nothing but cover her face with her hands and cry into them as quietly as she could manage. If anyone noticed her tears, they left her alone with them.

For a while.

And then there was a man sitting next to her, and a voice said, "Now, now, Gena. This isn't good."

She took her hands from her face and there was Sweetie Pie at her feet. The voice belonged to Paul Brackman, of course, because who else in this park knew her name? And he was handing her a handkerchief. A man's handkerchief, big enough to hold all her tears. She took the handkerchief, glanced sideways at him, and then without a word, not even a "thank you," covered her face with the handkerchief and turned away, profoundly embarrassed to be seen in such an exposed emotional state.

Paul said nothing while she blew her nose and dried her tears. She was still looking away from him, and with the bunched-up, sodden handkerchief clutched in both her hands, she said, "I'm so sorry. I feel so dumb."

"It's none of my business," he said. His voice was calm and quiet. "But I'm here, if you feel like talking."

She shook her head. How could she tell this man, whom she hardly knew, of the devastating scene she'd just been through? Devastating, and so humiliating!

"That bad, huh?"

"Yes. Every bit that bad." Now she managed a small smile. "But you're kind to offer." She looked down at her hands. "I've made a mess of your handkerchief. I'm sorry."

He smiled, a nice big smile. "Then you'll have to wash it first, before you give it back."

"Yes, I'll wash it." She laughed a little. "I'll even iron it."

"That sounds very domestic. Are you a domestic sort of woman?"

"Hardly. I suppose I can add being non-domestic to the list of my many inadequacies." She stuffed it into the back pocket of her jeans.

Paul said, "Why don't we take a walk, maybe get you a cup of coffee and see if we can find some tissues."

"I must look a mess."

He laughed. "I'm sure you've seen better days." He stood up. "Come on. Let's collect the dogs and get out of here."

A couple of calls brought the dogs over, and when she picked up Wiley, Gena said, "I'll have to carry him. I left without bringing his leash."

"I'm guessing you and the boyfriend had a lover's quarrel?"

"Felt more like a fight. Let's not talk about it."

"Suits me. We can talk about the weather. Or the state of the union. Or whatever you like. I just want to see a smile back on that pretty face."

Chapter Twenty-four

"Let's walk over to Madison," Paul said as they headed toward the park's exit. "First we'll get you some Kleenex. Then we can find a place with outside seating so we can tie up the dogs and get a cup of coffee. And talk about the weather."

The steadying calm of his voice and his easy manner were a blessing. Even though these last days had been so busy, and she'd been running since six this morning with no rest, she'd been feeling wonderful, so very pleased with her work and proud of herself. And then it was all spoiled by the sudden turmoil with Warren. No wonder she was an emotional mess, to say nothing of her face being red with weeping and her eyes swollen and unsightly.

Thank goodness Paul Brackman seemed able to take it all in stride. At a corner newsstand he bought her a packet of tissues and then suggested they walk down to the Graydon Hotel, where the restaurant had tables outside during the summer months.

"I'm sure I can get someone there to produce a leash for Wiley," he said. "The concierge probably keeps a couple of extras for guests."

It was a short walk. The evening was lovely, the rapid daytime pace had slowed to a more leisurely stroll, and she was glad of an excuse to stay away from home, and Warren, a little longer. Her mood lifted. She began to feel less scattered and unhappy.

"Would you like me to carry Wiley?" Paul asked. "Maybe he's getting heavy?"

"No. He's a comfort. I like holding him close."

"Lucky dog," Paul said. She gave him a surprised glance. He smiled, reassuringly, and said, "What I mean is, I always think dogs know when they're needed, and I'm guessing Wiley is glad he's helping you."

At the restaurant, Paul asked the waiter to get a leash from the hotel's concierge, and with the dogs secured next to them, tied up to the decorative barriers that separated diners from sidewalk passersby, Gena and Paul settled into the comfy seats and considered the menus the waiter handed them.

"Just coffee for me," Paul said to the waiter. He looked questioningly at Gena. "Have you had dinner?"

"Oh, God. I hadn't even thought. I'd been so busy today…had a meeting at noon so I missed lunch and then worked straight through. And then—" she paused. She couldn't speak of that awful scene with Warren. "And then, no. No dinner." She thought of the bag of Chinese food sitting on the coffee table back at the apartment, and her stomach growled politely at the thought. "Actually, I just realized, I've had nothing since a couple of doughnuts and coffee on the way back from Connecticut, and that was early this morning. I must be starved and didn't realize it. In fact, I *am* starved, and I *did* just realize it."

"Well then, no wonder you're feeling a little unsteady—going all day on an empty stomach. A couple of doughnuts and a cup of coffee. Didn't your mother tell you the first meal of the day should be a hearty one? To get you through the rigors of the day." He gave her a nice smile and then said, "Order up. Have a steak or whatever. You'll feel much better. And then you can tell me what you were doing in Connecticut so early in the morning."

"I don't have any money with me."

"Oh, come on." His smile turned into a laugh. "I'm rich enough. Have whatever you want."

Gena laughed, too. "I figured," she said. "And I will have a steak." To the waiter she added, "Rare. And the mashed potatoes and a salad on the side, and any green vegetable the chef recommends."

"Wine?" Paul asked.

"Why not. Whatever you choose." The prospect of a full meal was already cheering her up.

Paul looked over the wine list and, with a nod to the waiter, indicated to him something listed there. "And bring some bread right away," he said, smiling. "The lady is starving. And hold my coffee till later."

"Of course, sir," said the waiter, and he disappeared.

"So," Paul said, sitting back in his chair, "tell me what you were doing in Connecticut."

She thought a minute, choosing how much to tell him. "Well," she said thoughtfully, "I was working on my Romy deVere story."

"That's a name I hadn't heard in ages, before you mentioned her the other day. She was well before my time. And certainly well before yours. But I've seen pictures, and she was an incredibly beautiful woman. And also something scandalous, I seem to recall."

"I think her scandalous days are well behind her now. But she's still beautiful. Ninety-seven years old and still beautiful. She's been living a little reclusively, in a sort of cabin in the woods up in the northeastern section of Connecticut, up near the Massachusetts border. In recent years, she'd begun painting and she's doing really wonderful work. She was showing it in a local gallery up there, very modestly, not promoting it at all. I think just for her own pleasure. And one of our people caught wind of it and thought *Lady Fair* should do a story."

"I'm impressed. That's a story with rich possibilities. New lives, new careers, new goals. Inspirational for everyone—not just older women. At any age, it's good to know there's plenty of life ahead of us. I congratulate you. It's going to be a good article."

As though on cue, the waiter arrived with their wine. They were both quiet while he first went through the brief ritual of getting Paul's approval before he poured. When he'd gone, Paul raised his glass.

It was like a toast to her and her story, and she nodded her head to thank him.

Then she took her first sip. And her eyes opened very wide.

"Oh!"

Paul smiled. "Nice, isn't it?"

The word "nice" was perhaps too modest for a Bordeaux that was on the wine list at two hundred and eighty-five dollars a bottle. And had she known, Gena might have wondered why a man she hardly knew would spend so much on dinner just to cheer her up.

"Nice? I never tasted anything like it." She was silent for a moment, trying to find the right words. Finally, she said, "It's like music." She thought another moment, then added, "It's like the opening bars of a Beethoven symphony. It just sings, bang! right through you."

"You sure do have a writer's way with words. I'm glad you like it."

She took another sip. "What is it?"

"It's one of my favorite Bordeaux—a Pomerol." Paul's smile said how pleased he was. Pleased and admiring. For though Gena couldn't know it, with his selection of the wine, and her reaction to it, he'd satisfied a question he had about her at the same moment that the busboy arrived with the basket of dinner rolls and a small dish of butter curls.

She really was very hungry, and she attacked the rolls enthusiastically. Paul apparently enjoyed watching her place a roll on her bread plate, transfer some butter onto it, break off bits of roll, butter it, gobble it down, and then repeat the whole ritual on a second roll.

He laughed as she finished off the second roll. "You're a grown woman," he said, "and it's none of my business, but are you leaving room for the steak?"

"Oh, don't worry," she said. "I always eat like a horse."

Which made Paul laugh even harder. That was one confession he'd never before heard from any woman. Now he was looking forward to seeing her eat—in fact—like a horse. And at that very moment, her dinner arrived.

She was ladylike about it, but despite the earlier tears and her obvious stress, she did indeed eat with a hearty and healthy appreciation of the good food on her plate. Paul let her go to it for a bit, and then he started the conversation again.

"So." He went back to the subject of her story. "Tell me some more about Romy deVere. I'll ask you the question people always ask about celebrities: what's she really like?"

Well, that was one place Gena wasn't going to go, not with all the secrets buried there. Her response was cagey. "Too early to talk about it. You'll just have to read the story when it's published. But I'm guessing you don't subscribe to *Lady Fair,* so you'll have to watch for it on the newsstands."

Paul saw the very subtle change that had passed over her face. He looked at her sort of sideways for a bit, and then he said, "You look like a very satisfied cat with a couple of canary feathers peeking out at the corner of your mouth."

She shook her head slightly. "That's a very roundabout way of saying I look as though I know something I'm not sharing. Well, as I said, you'll have to read the story." Then she shrugged, as though to say she couldn't possibly care less. "But I think you're a man who doesn't read women's magazines. So you'll never know."

With that, she cut and popped into her mouth a perfect bit of juicy rare steak, and smiled around it at him.

"Hm," he said. "As I said. A very satisfied cat. I guess I will have to read that story, even if it is in a women's magazine. I can see I won't hear any more about that tonight. So tell me, how's the story on Sonny Gaile?"

She chewed down some more steak and took another sip of the wine.

Paul's glass was empty and the waiter appeared like magic to refill it.

"There aren't any secrets buried in that story, too, are there?" He sipped his wine, looked at her over the rim of his glass, then, abruptly wide-eyed, he set the glass down. He laughed. "There it is again. Another little yellow feather, just peeking out." He reached across the table and touched a fingertip lightly to the corner of her mouth. "Right there," he said. "You're keeping a whole slew of secrets, aren't you?"

She was abashed. She hadn't realized how transparent she was. Because of course, yes, the Sonny Gaile story had its big secret, too.

I'm going to have to develop a poker face. They should teach you that in journalism school.

She tried to look noncommittal. "I guess you'll have to read that story, too. But remember, *Lady Fair* does not do tabloid journalism. What we write is legitimate."

"I will look forward to it. I really will. Women's magazine or not, I'll watch for your pieces. Sonny Gaile and Romy deVere." He said the names as though he was entering them into his database.

And with that, they set aside the topic of Gena's work. For another hour, they chatted lightly about the weather, about local politics, about where she went to school, and how she came to be working at *Lady Fair*. He wanted to know why she'd been at his sister's home that day, and she explained about finding Wiley abandoned in the rain and needing to learn more about the breed, and he told her about his sister's interest in Crested dogs, and that Sweetie Pie was from a line of best-in-show winners, but that the breed had not yet made it to the top of the ladder, not yet having placed well enough at the annual Westminster Kennel Club show.

"Now there's a cause you could take on: promote the popularity of Chinese Cresteds. They're not very well-known and some people don't like their looks. Too bad. I think they're really very elegant. Look at the Pie, there. And your Wiley." Gena and Paul both looked down at the two dogs, who were sitting together most companionably, seeming to be having their own sociable evening, "chatting" to each other and watching the passing scene. "Two versions of the same dog, and both damned good-looking, I'd say."

How could she not appreciate his obviously genuine interest in her work, in her life, in her concerns? He listened quietly, attentive to her. With his hand folded, a rest for his chin, or gesturing lightly, emphasizing his comments.

Nice hands, she thought. And she enjoyed watching his face as he talked and was tickled by his wry enthusiasms. *A nice face. Very grown-up and intelligent. Nice gray eyes. Nice dark hair, expensive haircut. Very nice smile. I like how he knows his way around. That was a killer wine.*

He was signaling for the waiter. "I'm ready for that coffee now." Turning to Gena, he said, "How about dessert?"

"Oh, yes," she said. "I'd love anything with ice cream."

"We could get you some profiteroles, and have them pile on some ice cream on top."

"Great. Sounds perfect. With plenty of chocolate sauce?"

"Sure." He gave her that sideways look again. "You're serious, aren't you?"

She didn't answer. Just looked at him quizzically.

"I thought you were kidding," he said. "Women are always worried about their diets. I thought you were putting me on."

"You're right about women and their diets. Everyone I know. But, no. I'm afraid I have the opposite problem." She made a face. "I think God threw me a curve. He gave me a metabolism that just gobbles up everything I eat. I try to put on some curves, but—"

And there she stopped. Remembering Warren and his complaints about her looks. She looked away and said, "Never mind. You don't want to hear all that. And I'm actually lucky. I love desserts, plenty of women wish they were me, and I have nothing at all to complain about."

He'd seen right through her, saw the sudden cloud that stopped her, knew some sort of nerve had been touched, and kindly let it go. To the waiter he said, "We'll both have the profiteroles with plenty of chocolate sauce, and ice cream on the side." To Gena he said, "What kind of ice cream?"

"Anything."

"Chocolate," he said to the waiter. "For both of us."

* * * *

He walked her back to her building and said goodnight to her on the sidewalk. "You're sure you're okay now? No more tears?"

"I'll be all right. Really." She looked up at the building. The forty-first floor was a long way up, and she knew she'd have to face Warren when she got there.

Paul's gaze had followed hers, and he surprised her with a touch on her arm. He was very close.

"Gena," he said, all serious now. "If you need help, if you want to talk, if I can do something—"

What a nice face he has. What nice eyes—

"Thank you, but I'm all right. Really." She looked up again, toward the forty-first floor. "He's probably already gone to bed." It seemed she didn't need to explain who "he" was. "I'll gorge on some more ice cream. Ice cream always helps," she said. "And you've been very kind. Thank you. Perhaps I'll see you again in the park."

"You'll see me again. I want my handkerchief back."

"Oh! Of course! I might not see you in the park. How can I get it back to you?"

"Oh, yes. Of course. In case I don't see you in the park." He took his wallet from the inside breast pocket of his suit jacket. "Here's my card. It has my home address and phone number. You can call me, if you like." He paused and glanced up along the building's façade. "Or if you need to. You know, if things don't go well, you can always call me."

Her hand went to her hair. It was the first time in the last couple of hours she remembered how disheveled she'd become.

"I'll be all right, I'm sure. I'm just embarrassed that I've been such a mess tonight."

He shook his head, as though not accepting what she was saying. "I understand," he said. "Life is so complicated, isn't it?" Then he smiled and said, "Don't forget. Call if you need to," and he and Sweetie Pie headed up Seventy-Third Street.

She watched them until they reached the corner and turned to go uptown.

She sighed a very big, very deep sigh.

She should have been troubled by how she felt—and perhaps that would come later—but there was no question about it, she was attracted to this man. A forbidden reaction to what had been, after all, only human kindness and generosity. But it was a very nice feeling. She sighed one more time, savoring the lovely feeling. She picked Wiley up and, hugging him close, she whispered into his long, pointy, softly feathered ear, "He really is a very nice man, don't you think?"

* * * *

It was already past eleven o'clock, and on the chance that Warren was already asleep, and because she'd left in such a state, she stopped at the desk and got the spare key from Alfie. And, sure enough, when she let herself into the apartment, all was dark.

But Warren wasn't there.

Not like Warren to leave just because he was mad at her, but it was just as well. She knew she looked a mess, and she hoped to get cleaned up and in bed before he got home.

But first, she got her phone from her bag. And with Paul's card still in her hand, she transferred the information into her contacts list.

Paul R. Brackman. 953 Fifth Avenue. New York, NY 10028.

And a telephone number. Just one. Cell? Landline? Nothing more.

She turned the card over in her hand, examining it. Heavy stock, engraved. Cream white. *Yes*, she thought. *It suits him. It goes with the very good suit and the very good haircut.*

She was examining it as the door opened and Warren came in. She slipped the card into her pocket.

He dropped his keys onto the little table next to the door. "Where'd you go?" he asked.

Wiley started to bark. She picked him up, shushing him.

"Out. We walked around."

This is how it begins, she thought. *Keeping secrets.*

He went into the bathroom. She waited, holding Wiley. Then he came out.

"Where have you been?" she asked.

"I went to a movie."

He went into the kitchen and took a beer out of the fridge.

She stood in the doorway while he drank the beer.

"We shouldn't fight, Warren."

He passed her to go into the living room. "And you shouldn't make me mad."

"You said some very mean things to me."

"Yeah, well maybe it's just the truth, and you don't want to hear it. I mean, look at you right now. Your hair is a mess, your eyes are all puffed up and red. And look what you're wearing." His glance slid disapprovingly over her jeans and shirt. "A guy likes to be able to show off his girl, you know?"

Funny, of all things, her mind went to that night she'd seen Paul and Cherie Blitz going into the restaurant.

It's true. A man must feel really good when he's seen with a really good-looking woman on his arm. Makes him look successful.

But still—

"Not everyone can be stunningly beautiful, Warren. And if you think about it, no one ever says a man has to be handsome. Let alone movie-star handsome. You're not bad looking, Warren, but it doesn't matter to me if you're not as gorgeous as a movie star."

"It's different for men. You know that. Everyone knows that." He headed into the bedroom. "Maybe you could take some lessons from the people you work with. I kinda thought that would happen when you went to work there." He was peeling off his clothes. "Anyway, I'm going to bed now. You think about it."

Gena knew she'd just been dismissed.

By the time she showered and was ready to turn out the light, Warren was asleep—or, at least, he seemed to be asleep, though when she got into the bed, she thought he shifted a bit so that their bodies did not touch.

Am I so awful he can't even be near me?

I don't think so.

I bet Paul doesn't turn away when he's in bed with a woman.

I wonder what Paul Brackman is like in bed.

She smiled into the dark room.

He does have such nice hands.

Chapter Twenty-five

She hadn't slept well, and she woke up with the feeling that maybe she had done something bad. Or was about to do something bad. Warren was already up, and she could hear him moving around in the kitchen. As she brushed her teeth and wound her hair up into a twisty bun, she asked her mirror self, "Is a little fantasy flirtation really so wicked?"

As she dressed, she kept up a running conversation with herself.

"Is it such a terrible thing just to imagine?"

She took a dress from the closet—a pretty thing, white, with a flowing line and a summery feel. It felt silky all over.

"And Warren made me feel so bad yesterday."

A black, brocaded bolero vest she hadn't worn for years was tucked away at the back of the closet, and she slipped it on over the dress.

"Why does he *do* that?"

Warren was in the kitchen, reading the *Wall Street Journal* and finishing his breakfast. For a moment, from the doorway, she watched him. He was apparently not aware she was there.

Finally, she asked him, "Warren, why do you do that?"

He looked up from the paper, got his attention focused on her, and said, "Do what?"

"Why do you make me feel so bad?"

He didn't even put down his coffee cup. "Oh, come on, honey. Let's not start off the morning with a sour face. I just said some things you didn't want to hear. For your own good. For both of us. Don't be mad." He finished his coffee and returned his attention to the paper. "I like that dress you're wearing. You should get more like that."

He did that so easily. Dismissed her.

* * * *

There's no anonymity like the anonymity a crowded subway car provides, and there's no privacy, either, that's comparable to the privacy afforded by a mob of strangers pressed up close, maintaining their own zone of personal, individual space. Fortunately, the fifteen-minute subway ride to work gave her a chance to start all over again.

"Why is it," she asked herself, "that Warren makes me feel bad?"

No answer arrived.

"And Paul makes me feel good?"

The train clattered on. People got on. People got off.

"What kind of girl has a boyfriend for years, ever since high school, lives with him in a great apartment he pays for, pretty much commits her life to him—and then has sexy fantasies about a man she hardly knows?"

She listened for an answer from her conscience, but no answer came back.

Her next question was a little bolder.

"Is a little fantasy flirtation really so bad?"

And still there was no answer.

She was at the halfway mark to work—Forty-Second Street, where the crowd thinned out and she found a seat.

"Is it such a terrible thing to just imagine—?"

And still her conscience remained silent.

"It's just fantasy. A daydream. Is that so bad?"

Apparently, her conscience had decided to be absent.

But in its place, a different voice was speaking to her.

Mind if I sit down?

It was Paul's voice, a voice in her fantasy, of course. And in her fantasy, her daydream, Paul took the vacant seat next to her. He was dressed less formally than usual. His collar was open and he wore no tie. His hair was a little windblown, but nice. Thick and dark and wavy, falling a bit over his forehead.

Continuing her fantasy, she smiled at him, letting him know she had no objection.

You look pretty today, he said.

This daydream had made a nice start.

Oh, this old thing.

They both laughed at the unsophisticated cliché.

I've been reading your Lady Fair *articles. You write well, Gena.*

I didn't know you had any interest in my work.

*It's you I have an interest in. I followed you when you left Wiley off at
Dog Prep this morning. I wanted to be sure you got to work safely.*

Would you like to come up to my office? See where I work?

That was part of my plan.

Her fantasy made him want to get her up to his apartment, but she
decided to hold him off.

*I have a full agenda today. Maybe you'd like to come along, keep me
company while I work.*

Only if you let me buy you lunch.

I'd like that. And then later—in her daydream, she let her expression
be suggestive—*later tonight, after work maybe*—

For the rest of the day, as she worked on the Romy deVere story, her
fantasy Paul stayed with her. He was looking over her shoulder as she
typed out:

The Character Is the Challenge, Not the Cheekbones

Good title, he said.

"Yes, it is," she said aloud. She sat quietly for a moment, thinking, her
fingers poised over the keyboard. And then she began to write.

"What happens to them, those former Hollywood stars, who once blazed
brilliantly in our film firmament? 'Is he still alive?' we ask when a name
comes up. Or, 'Didn't she die in a fire? Or maybe it was a car crash?' And
when we learn that no, he—or she—is still very much alive, we may feel
a disappointment, for it seems unreasonable, as though against some law
of nature. Stars should die in a blaze of glorious flame. It is too sad to
think that out of the public's view they merely age, grow wrinkled and
gray, become feeble and lose their brilliance."

Gena stopped, lifted her fingertips from the keyboard, thought for a
moment, and then, almost without further pause except to refer to her
written and transcribed notes, wrote like a demon, taking only occasional
sips from the coffee cup Selma had silently placed on her desk.

She didn't look at her watch until it was past time for lunch. She
contemplated what she had done so far, and was pleased. Thousands of
words, and good ones. This was going to be a good story.

Yes, it will be. I told you, you do good work.

Her fantasy self gave him a nod, a wink, and a smile. She had imagined
him with her the whole time, and in her imagination he had walked around

the room, helping her think things through; he'd looked over her shoulder, he'd asked questions that she needed to answer. His collaboration had kept her moving steadily along. She put her head back and her imaginary Paul put a light, imaginary kiss on her lips. With one hand—one of those nice hands—he undid the twisty bun of dark hair and let it fall to her shoulders. And they both smiled. Co-conspirators. He was a product of her own mind, she knew that perfectly well. But gee, it sure was fun.

Instead of going out for lunch, she ordered in a roast beef sandwich, a banana, a toasted and buttered corn muffin, and a chocolate shake. While the deli man took her order, she put her hand to her hair. The twisty bun was still in place, which seemed sad.

For the next hour, there was a flurry of phone activity, and her fantasy man took a fantasy walk while she handled messages, questions, and requests, while at the same time eating her lunch. When things quieted down, she put aside the Romy story to let it "cook" for a while and turned to the New York dogs idea. She brought up her notes from that Sunday planning session almost two weeks ago and gave the list a quick glance.

> *2. Pitch something to Marge about a New York dogs story.*
> *Rich dogs/poor dogs? Lifestyles*
> *Westminster Kennel Club—dog show. (When?)*
> *Dog fashion, accessories, costs (range? fancy—plain)*
> *Costs, generally.*
> *Laws?*
> *Homeless?*
> *Compare—city dogs, suburban, country?*
> *Do city dogs suffer, confined to apartments? (Really?)*

She looked over the list thoughtfully. Each item could be a full, stand-alone story. Then, with a big smile, she added another item.

> *Owner(s) at work—day care for dogs?*

"Thank goodness for East Side Dog Prep and Day Care," she said to the empty room. "And thank you, Paul, for making it possible. I'll have to find a way to thank you."

I look forward to that. He was laughing. *Did you think I'd gone away?*
She laughed, too. She was enjoying this.

He listened in when she made her first call to Grover Simms, the communications director of the Westminster Kennel Club, and made an appointment to meet with him the next morning. Paul approved when she selected, out of a long roster of attorneys who advertised themselves online as dog law specialists, a likely sounding woman named Elizabeth Woofley who had published a textbook for use in law school classes on animal law. Ms. Woofley's offices were on Madison Avenue, not far from the Westminster offices, and she said her calendar was clear for an hour tomorrow at one o'clock and she'd be delighted to talk to a writer from *Lady Fair*. He looked jealous when a call to Dr. Zweig produced a hearty, "Ah, yes, my dear. Yes, of course. Come by on Saturday morning. Early, if possible." He laughed as she combed through the offerings of insanely expensive accessories for the dogs of the very, very rich and made a list of pet accessory boutiques that deserved a visit. And he was sympathetic when she called the Coalition for the Homeless and arranged to meet with their press person to learn about the life of a homeless dog. Sometimes she saw a homeless person with a dog, always a devoted dog, sitting on a blanket or on a large cardboard box opened out to form a mat, and she wanted to explore the stories at the other end of the social spectrum.

* * * *

This was her work for the next two days. She visited rescue locations and spent time with a lovely woman at the Humane Society who sat with her in the reception area and patiently answered all her questions as cats and dogs were brought in and out, some on leashes, some in carriers, some in arms. She examined dog accessories at a dozen pet shops. She gathered information on legislation affecting dogs, and she met with people in the Central Park Conservancy to learn more about the park's off-leash areas—there are twenty-nine—and she interviewed a homeless man on Third Avenue whose big camel-colored dog lay quietly beside him on a tattered blanket of indeterminate color and pattern. The dog rested his head on his paws. "I don't always get a meal," the man told her, "but the dog eats before I do."

Through all her field research, her fantasy Paul stayed off in the distance. But she knew she could get him back whenever she needed to.

In the meantime, Warren was so busy at work she hardly saw him. And when Sunday came, he said he had another golf date with the boss, and would be gone all day. She began to wonder if—was it possible—could he be seeing someone else? She talked to Viv about it.

"Oh, honey. What's the difference? Golf or another girl, he's not with you." They were relaxing with a late-afternoon glass of wine at Tavern on the Green. "But I've said all I have to say on the subject of Warren Haglund. You know I love you no matter what you do about him."

* * * *

It wouldn't have been possible to avoid the real-life Paul forever, and indeed, there he was, not at all a fantasy, sitting on a bench at the dog park while Sweetie Pie visited sedately with the other dogs. He smiled at her across the park, and she walked over to join him. She removed Wiley's leash and watched him race several laps around the space before he settled down with the other dogs.

She felt transparent, as though by some magic he'd be able to see what she'd been thinking of him. It didn't help that he was dressed almost as she'd imagined him in her daydreams: shirt open at the collar, no tie, no jacket, his shirt sleeves rolled up. His hair looked nice but not so neat. She restrained the impulse to run her hand over his hair, to tidy it a bit.

"You look pretty today," he said.

"Oh, this old thing," she said, and they both laughed.

"I've been thinking about you," he said.

Now she really felt transparent. But he was not a fantasy and this was not a daydream.

"Tomorrow night," he said. "There's a concert tomorrow night, here in the park. Dogs allowed. Would you like—"

She stopped him with a gesture.

"Thanks, but I can't. I'm going to be out of town tomorrow. On an assignment. And won't be back till really late. So sorry. It would have been fun."

"Maybe another time," he said. It was impossible to tell if he intended anything by the suggestion, and they chatted lightly after that. Gena felt so silly having laid all her romantic feelings on Paul Brackman, while Paul Brackman was really only a dog care surrogate, taking care of his sister's Sweetie Pie while she was away, and there was nothing between them except the care of their dogs.

Which was odd, because while they'd sat together, hadn't she absolutely felt something totally primal and magnetic, like a current of electricity, running between them?

She tried to be sensible and grown-up, she really did, but he was such a nice man, and he made her feel good.

And she was wearing that pretty white dress, with the black brocaded bolero. And he'd said she looked pretty.

Chapter Twenty-six

On the plane to Knoxville, the camera people were feeling more jovial than usual. By that time they'd all been informed about Sonny's wedding. They'd signed all the nondisclosure papers, and there was an air of adventure and conspiracy about the whole trip. Nell Magano was sitting with her hair-and-makeup crew, and a couple of rows away from the others, Gena was sitting by herself with an empty seat next to her. Her mood had been fairly somber for the last few days, and she was just as glad to be separated from the rest so she wouldn't be forced to join in the festive spirit.

And it really was a festive spirit. They were going to a wedding, after all, a wedding that was going to make news. Everyone seemed so bubbly, you'd think they'd already started on the champagne. But Ira Garlen, whose gift and genius it was to see what lay behind the masks people put between themselves and the rest of the world, had seen the pain Gena was hiding. Ira had worked with Gena for a couple of years, and he'd come to like the young woman and want a good future for her. He'd met the boyfriend once at the magazine's Christmas party, and he wasn't sure how that was going to work out.

An ambitious young man, he'd thought, *but doesn't appreciate the charms of the girl he's with.*

"Hey, Gena. Mind if I join you?" The plane had reached cruising altitude and people were moving around.

"Of course not." She removed the papers and the magazine she'd put next to her to clear the seat for Ira. "Always a pleasure." She stuffed the papers into the back pocket of the seat in front of her. "The weather forecast is good for this shoot today. I understand they're planning to have the ceremony outdoors, at sunset, with the glow on the mountains behind them."

"They forwarded pictures. I think we've got it under control."

"You always do. You're the best, Ira. You really are."

Ira said nothing, just acknowledged the compliment with a little nod and a small smile.

"I met Sonny once," he said. "Nice young man. Couple of years ago. He was in New York for a business meeting. He was coming in, I was going out. We were introduced, we chatted for a couple of minutes. When I called him to make arrangements about this shoot today, he remembered me. Remembered where we'd met, what we talked about." Ira paused for a moment, savoring the memory. "Not an ounce of ego about that boy. And nice manners."

"I had the same impression," Gena said. "I liked his partner, too. Tim. I bet they're going to make a very good marriage." And then she added, "Of course, you never know..."

Ira noted the cloud that passed over her face, and he saw the sadness that darkened her eyes.

"No, you never do know," he said. "Really good marriages are so rare."

They sat silently. Ira took the magazine out of the pocket and leafed through it. Gena gazed at the clouds outside. After a little while, she turned to Ira.

"Ira, you've photographed the most beautiful women in the world. You've talked to them. You must have gotten to know them at least a little. Maybe a lot. You've seen them in every state of dress and undress. They can't possibly have any secrets from you."

"Everyone has secrets, Gena." Ira smiled like a wise old owl.

"Well, maybe you can tell me: What is their secret? How do they do it? I see them sometimes, around the office. When they're not all 'camera ready.' Sometimes they don't even look pretty. Is it some kind of magic you do? With lights? With makeup?"

Ira was beginning to get an idea of what was troubling Gena.

"That's part of it," he said. "Lights. Shadows. Makeup. Camera angles. That part is obvious. Those are the things we do to them. Then there's what they were born with. The good forehead. The wide-set eyes. The cheekbones. But you know all that."

"Yes. I know all that."

"But also, Gena, these women are self-selected. Somewhere along the way, when they were girls, they looked in the mirror and told themselves that being professionally beautiful was something they wanted to do. And then they believed they could do it. It isn't just a matter of imitating what they've seen on the runway or in the magazines. They bring an attitude, a confidence, something very hard to define, but it's something I try to capture with my camera. Partly, it's practice. Partly, it's training. Like everything else, mastering the craft. Doing it a thousand times. Becoming a professional. And partly, it's a mystery. Like all art, it's a mystery."

This was Ira's favorite subject, and he was about to expound further, but one of the camera people came over and said they needed him to consult about a technical problem, something about timing the sunset to coordinate with the ceremony.

He cast a glance at Gena and decided she'd just as soon be left alone, so he whispered quickly to her, "If you'd like to talk, Gena, anytime—" But she gestured to him, "No, I'm fine," so he left her alone.

Brittney was waiting when they landed, with a fleet of vans to take them to the cabin. She greeted Gena with hugs and air-kisses and kept up a running chatter all the way to the cabin, about the plans for the day, the bridegrooms' excitement, their writing of their vows, the gorgeous wedding cake Mrs. Wilkins had made, and thank goodness the weather was cooperating! Gena was thankful for Brittney's bubbling effusions— they created a distraction that allowed her to deflect any attention away from herself.

At the cabin, the camera people immediately spread out according to their prearranged plans for photographing the various stages of the day's activities. Mrs. Wilkins had people in to help her with food, and Linus came up from the horse barn to help with setting up tables and chairs. Only the closest friends and relatives would be there for the wedding, and all had been sworn to the most solemn secrecy. The weather prediction was for perfect blue skies and gentle breezes, and everything about the day promised a life of happily ever after.

Sonny and Tim had gone off to their separate rooms, determined not to see each other before the ceremony. They'd agreed earlier to allow Gena a little time with each of them and do a very simple interview, so she went into Tim's room first. She found him sitting near the window, in a big wing chair that was covered in a blue and white crewel fabric. He was gazing across the green hills toward the mountains, and he turned to greet her as she entered the room.

"Gena. Our recording angel. Welcome." He gestured broadly toward the serene view. "Could we possibly have arranged a more perfect day?"

"You both deserve it," she said. "I'm so happy for you. And I won't take much time. I suppose you want to be alone with your thoughts." She got out a notepad and pencil. "Brittney told me your dad is going to be performing the ceremony."

"Yes. He and my mom got here last night. They're staying in a hotel in Merryville, and Brittney's gone to pick them up. They should be here in time for lunch. They've never met Sonny, so they'll get to spend some time with him this afternoon. Sonny and I swore we wouldn't see each other all day today, until we meet at the altar. I don't know why we both wanted to do that, except somehow it just seemed right. A little theatrical, maybe, heightening the suspense. Gives me time to think about my vows." He gestured toward a sheet of paper on a nightstand next to the bed.

He knew what she would want to ask. "They're not for publication, Gena. So I'm not going to share what I've written."

"Of course. I understand." She looked longingly over at the paper, thinking that the men's vows would be a great addition to the story. "I understand," she repeated. "And," she said, changing the subject, "what will you be wearing?"

"Oh, God! We went back and forth on that. Must have spent three days trying to decide. Between traditional, casual, formal, flamboyant. We wanted to honor the event by being traditional and solemn in matching tuxedos, we wanted to be extravagant by wearing white tie and tails with striped pants, we wanted to express our creativity by wearing something totally made up for the occasion, we wanted to assert our individuality by not wearing identical outfits, we wanted to outrage everyone by wearing jeans and T-shirts."

Gena was laughing. "And what did you decide on?"

He gestured toward the closet, where a gray suit was hanging on the doorknob.

"Matching suits, no vest, solid color silk ties, but my favorite color is blue so my pocket square is blue and Sonny's is red."

"So you're not exactly a matched set."

"No, but close. An exact match wouldn't be good. Sonny is not my alter ego. And I'm not his. But he adds something precious to my life. He adds love. And beauty. He is a beautiful man and I cherish him for that."

That, she thought, is worth a quote, so she made a discreet note, and then went on to dig a little deeper into Tim's background. They talked about his childhood, his work before he met Sonny, how he and Sonny met, their shared interests, their differences. She spent a half hour with him, and then went off to find Sonny.

"He's in his room," the houseboy said. "Writing his vows."

She knocked once, but there was no answer.

Perhaps, she thought, *he doesn't want to be disturbed.* She knocked one more time, gently, just in case.

"Yeah, it's okay. Come on in."

She found him at the writing table on the opposite side of the room, facing the bed. He was working at a laptop, and he looked very much like a man struggling to find the right words.

"I thought this would be easy. Hello, Gena. You're a writer. I need help."

"Oh, no. No way I'm going to help you write your wedding vows. That's got to be all yours. But you're a great writer, Sonny. Look at all the wonderful songs you've done. You don't need any help from me."

"That's what I thought when I sat down to do this. And guess what: it's harder than I thought it was going to be."

"Funny. I just said hello to Tim and he's got his all done."

"Can you give me a hint?"

"No way. Anyway, he wouldn't show me what he'd written. But you couldn't go wrong with love and beauty."

"Love and beauty. They go together, don't they?"

"I wouldn't know." The words slipped out, and she was instantly sorry.

Sonny swiveled around in his chair and studied her face. "That sounds sad. What's up? Do you want to talk?"

"Not at all. This is your day, Sonny. And I'm here only to help you preserve it. For the record. For the public. So I'll just ask you a few questions and then I'll leave you alone and let you concentrate on preparing your vows."

She had pencil and paper ready, and for about twenty minutes she asked about their plans for the day (champagne for everyone after the ceremony and then a quiet dinner with just family and a couple of old friends), any thoughts about a family (much too soon to know, but it's definitely been talked about), whether they had honeymoon plans (a quick trip incognito to New York to see a couple of shows, walk around, see some sights, then back to work for both of them, with a new album coming out in a month and a European tour starting in ten days).

"Now I'll leave you," she said. "See you after the ceremony. I'll just wander around, see what I can see, and try not to get in anyone's way."

* * * *

She spent the next couple of hours nosing around, picking up what bits of color she could, asking questions, taking notes, using her cell phone's camera. A makeshift patio had been set up on a green and beautifully landscaped space near the cabin, where the view of the mountains, veiled in their blueish haze, would create an inspiring sunset-tinted backdrop for the wedding couple. Sonny and Tim had apparently decided against any stagecraft. There were no flower decorations, no ornamental arch. Not even an altar. Yet the natural shrubbery and trees formed a beautiful frame against the mountains.

She wandered down the hill to the horse barn, a good half a mile away from all the wedding activity. Linus was up at the house, and there was no one with the horses. She walked silently through the barn, past the stalls, and out to the pasture. And there was Belinda. Oh, such a strange looking animal she was! In all her multicolored, randomly marked glory. And yet—

And yet—

—there was something beautiful about her.

She loped over to Gena and reached her long face toward her, as though expecting a bit of carrot or apple. Gena held out her open, empty hands.

"Sorry, Belinda. I have nothing for you."

But Belinda showed no sign of disappointment. She was an affectionate animal, and she nuzzled Gena's neck softly.

"I wonder what it is Sonny sees in you."

She tried to see the horse though Sonny's eyes. She remembered what Brittney had told her about how she'd just appeared out of the woods, all skinny and sad, when Sonny was just a kid and he took her in and loved her—and his love made her beautiful in his eyes. And as Belinda loped away across the pasture, Gena took a good look at the funny looking animal and saw that she really was beautiful, because she was loved. And Gena began to cry.

* * * *

It was almost time for the wedding to begin, so Gena pulled herself together and walked back to where everything was set and ready. In a half hour, the sun would be casting the perfect glow onto the mountains, and Ira's crew, working unobtrusively and efficiently, had everything in place to make a discreet yet gorgeous record of the event. The few guests, including Brittney and Linus and Mrs. Wilkins and Sonny's and Tim's parents, were drifting out to the seats that had been set up for them. Gena placed herself in a back row, apart from the guests who had a closer connection to the wedding couple.

She was writing her notes and using her cell camera when Tim's father went up to the front. He had some prepared comments in his hands and was looking them over. People were filling the seats. A young man, who turned out to be one of Sonny's younger brothers, took a position near the side, framed by great banks of white spirea. He had a guitar strapped across his chest and he began to play softly. The sun was beginning to give the mountain a golden glow, and at a signal—Gena couldn't tell from where—he began to play and hum the song that Sonny had sung so beautifully at that London concert, "You Are So Beautiful."

And at another signal, Sonny and Tim came from the house and walked together to the front. The quiet chatter became silent, the guitar player stopped playing, and only the twilight roosting song of birds in a nearby tree could be heard. The sun's light on the hills grew more intense and Tim's father began to speak. "We are gathered here today..." Gena stopped writing on her notepad, turned off her phone, and put it away. Ira Garlen had schooled his people well: they did their job so skillfully and so discreetly, they disturbed no one.

There is a magic to a wedding that softens even the most jaded and most cynical of guests. At least, Gena liked to think so, and she gave herself heart and soul to the experience. She looked upon the two grooms with an affection that belied the short time and the limited shared experience she'd had with them. She felt respect for the very private group of family and the few friends who were gathered to witness, support, and surround these two men with their love and protection. She even cried a tear or two, for how hard-hearted must a woman be to shed no tear at a wedding? She smiled, because this time she'd come prepared for tears and she had a couple of pretty handkerchiefs in her bag. One of them even had a bit of lace decorating the edges.

From where she sat, she was able to see the grooms' faces. Tim was clearly aware of the solemnity and engrossed in the joy of the event. But Sonny, so much younger, looked almost ethereal, as though he expected to be wafted into the heavens at any moment. Gena smiled, pleased to have had a glimpse into such innocence. And she said a bit of a prayer that they be able to preserve so profound a state of love throughout a lifetime.

Sonny and Tim are special. They might just be able to do it.

As they spoke their vows, about the love and beauty they'd each found in the other (as it turned out, they'd created almost identical vows), Gena found herself falling into a daydream: There was a wedding and she was the bride, standing there before the minister. At first she dressed her fantasy self in a shimmery gray silk suit, exquisitely tailored, modeled a bit on the suits Sonny and Tim were wearing. With serious jewelry. Platinum, she decided. But then she discarded that choice. No point in imitating the men before her. No, something quite different? Something traditional? Frothy white? Like the princess dolls from her childhood? With exquisite lace and masses of tulle. And pearls everywhere. Or maybe something sleek and very modern, very form-fitting. No, she discarded that one—she'd look like a stick, a white, shiny stick. Somehow, she imagined the minister in dove gray with white gloves. Definitely dove gray with white gloves. Surrounded by banks of flowers, and it would not be outdoors—no, it would be in a chapel and it would be a conventional wedding, with a harpist and a traditional reception afterward, and it would be the most perfect, loveliest day of her life. All the magical arts would have been applied and she would have been made into a beauty, and the minister would speak the most inspiring words, and they would speak their vows with genuine inspiration, she and the man standing there by her side, and as her fantasy self turned to smile at her fantasy groom, Gena's fantasizing self woke abruptly from her daydream, for without a word of permission, totally unbidden, the fantasy had placed Paul R. Brackman of 953 Fifth Avenue next to her at her fantasy altar. He stood there next to her imaginary self, as real as if he were real. With his nice smile, and his nice gray eyes and his nice hands, and the tiniest bit of gray at the temples and looking perfectly groomed and utterly at home in her wishful thinking.

Did ever a subconscious thought come crashing up to the surface with such explosive force?

What could I have been thinking?!

Stunned and embarrassed by where her fantasy had taken her, she totally lost track of what was going on around her. Rings were exchanged, but Gena didn't see it happen, the final pronouncement of a marriage was made but she never heard it, and the kiss that symbolized the end and the beginning, which she'd meant to catch with her cell phone camera, remained unrecorded by her. Gena's attention had been wrenched away from the real wedding of Sonny Gaile and Tim Fine and was focused solely on the unsettling revelation she'd just experienced.

At first, Gena wrote off Paul's sudden appearance in her fantasy as a bit of errant brain chemistry. Maybe it was some sort of associative trick, the gray of the men's suits with the gray of Paul's eyes, or the bit of gray at his temples. Or perhaps it could be blamed on the glass of wine she'd had earlier. Glass and a half, actually. Or had she eaten something odd, something that caused hallucinations, perhaps a morsel of some unacceptable mushroom in the soup Mrs. Wilkins served at lunch? She thought of Dickens's Scrooge, trying to argue Marley's ghost away by blaming his appearance, chains and all, on something he'd eaten, "an undigested bit of beef…a crumb of cheese…"

But she knew that it wasn't something she'd eaten that made Paul Brackman appear as a phantom groom in her idle daydreaming. And she also knew that she couldn't let that happen again.

"Just forget about it," she told herself. "It doesn't mean anything." She didn't hear her ego's tiny, all-wise voice:

Yeah, right!

* * * *

Around her, the crew was quickly and quietly packing up their gear. They wouldn't be staying for the dinner, and neither would she. While they packed and the remaining guests milled about, chatting and slowly moving toward the dinner tables, Gena went into the house and found a bathroom, where she could splash some cold water on her face and pull herself together. She locked the door, then looked into the mirror and had a little conversation with herself. "Gena, you hardly know the man. Don't be an idiot."

She gave herself a couple of minutes to convince herself she was ready to join the others.

And on the plane, flying over the tip of the Chesapeake Bay, she said to herself, "You're a grown woman. Schoolgirl crushes are for schoolgirls. And you're no schoolgirl. You have a full-grown man in your bed at home, a man you've been living with for almost five years now, and who might well be your husband one of these days."

And again she told herself, "So don't be an idiot. Don't do something ridiculous."

How much pressure does it take to force an unruly subconscious thought back into its underground psychic lair?

* * * *

It was almost three a.m. when her taxi left her off at Two Twelve East Seventy-Third, and she was exhausted. She couldn't possibly think about anything. She peeled off her clothes, didn't even wash her face, and fell into bed. She noticed for the littlest second that Warren wasn't there, but work sometimes kept him at the office till all hours and she was too tired to give it more than a second's thought. Ambitious New Yorkers don't believe in "early to bed," and car services do a brisk business bringing them home at all hours. She hoped he wouldn't wake her when he rolled in.

Chapter Twenty-seven

Warren, at least, was not a fantasy. When she woke up, he was in the kitchen, reading the morning paper and drinking coffee. From a Starbucks cup, she noted.

"Did you just get in?"

"We pulled an all-nighter. I slept on the couch in the office. Just came home to shower and change."

"How's the project going?"

"Terrific. We keep this up, we'll bring it in ahead of schedule."

"So you must be winning points with management."

"Yep." And he went back to reading the paper.

"Well, I'm going to dress. Gotta get to the office."

But he was already engrossed in an article on currency shifts and didn't hear her.

And in the shower, she was reviewing the situation.

"This isn't good. I don't think Warren cares if I'm dead or alive."

Then, brushing her teeth, "He stays out all night, and then doesn't even ask when did I get home or how was the trip, or how's the story going."

And, pulling on a pair of skinny black jeans, high heeled booties, and a voluminous multicolored top belted low over her hips, "Like he said, there are plenty of other girls who'd be happy to take my place. Prettier girls. Sexier girls."

And for the many-thousandth time in her life, Gena sized up the image of herself in the mirror and found herself too broad-mouthed, too wide-eyed, too wild-haired, too many things that were too much. Except body fat, of which there was too little.

She could spray some hairspray on her hair to keep it tidier, but there was nothing to be done about the big mouth, the teeth that showed like a row of headlights when she smiled, the eyebrows that, despite plucking, waxing, threading, and everything else she'd tried, continued to look altogether too dramatic. Right on the edge of fierce, she thought. Oh, how she envied those wispy, pale girls with the delicate-looking bones, who looked so fragile. They obviously needed to be handled gently. By big, strong, manly men.

She made a face at herself in the mirror, and, for the many-thousandth time, she pulled herself together, picked herself up off the mat once more, gathered up her things, and left for work.

Warren was still reading the paper as she closed the door behind her. She'd said goodbye, but he was too engrossed to notice.

* * * *

At the office, there was plenty to keep her mind busy. Her collection of notes on Sonny and the wedding now filled more than one folder and needed careful sorting. That took up most of the morning, and then, without a proper break for lunch, only an ordered-in club sandwich and a milkshake at her desk, she began outlining the story, which she was filing under the temporary working title, "You Are So Beautiful."

Keeping her mind busy was important, because when she didn't keep it occupied, it kept sliding around to what would happen after work, when she went to pick Wiley up from Dog Prep. Would she perhaps run into Paul? And if not tonight, maybe tomorrow morning? Or, in any case, inevitably, sometime soon? And was she eager for that to happen? Or, as her better angels seemed to be telling her, was that absolutely a no-no?

Had she been caught in the snare of a momentary attraction—it could happen to anyone—or was there really something special, something worth holding on to, about this man? Was it only because she happened to be going through a rough patch with Warren and was more vulnerable than she should be? Didn't she have an obligation to work things out with Warren? Think how many years there were between them. And how could there be any real attraction to Paul? She hardly knew anything at all about him. Shouldn't relationships be built on common interests, shared values, the careful work of getting to know each other on a deep and significant level? At an intimate level?

Whoops!

"Intimate" was the wrong word. It took her right back to her sexualized fantasies about Paul, and that was just where she absolutely must not—didn't want to—go.

This whole emotional turmoil about Paul, the moral dilemma wrapped around a preoccupation that she just couldn't shake, had her in a state by the time she got herself uptown and to the doors of Dog Prep. And, of course, when she entered, there he was. Right as she walked in, he was picking up Sweetie Pie and chatting with Labibbah, the pretty young woman who worked at the reception desk. Paul turned as Gena came in, and he was just as attractive, standing there so casually, tall and at ease, holding Sweetie Pie's leash with one nice hand and signing some papers on Labibbah's desk with his other nice hand. Gena felt her cheeks burn, and she knew she was blushing with embarrassment, as though anyone, and Paul in particular, could know what her thoughts about him had been. But, of course, he didn't know, and he merely said, "Hi," and turned back to the papers he was signing.

She caught her breath. She put on the conventional show of nonchalance. "Hi," she said. And to Labibbah she said, "I've come to get Wiley. Has he been okay?"

"He's been such a treat. That little boy is just so much fun. And he and Sweetie Pie here are best friends. They get along like they've know each other forever. Wait a minute. I'll call Nikki to get him." And she picked up the phone at her desk and told Nikki that Wiley's owner was there to pick him up.

In a minute, she was ready to leave, and Paul was waiting for her at the door.

"Mind if I walk with you?"

"Not at all," she said. Her heart was beating fast, and it was hard to look at him directly. "I was going to walk with Wiley for a while anyway. I haven't seen him since yesterday morning."

I feel fourteen years old. This is ridiculous.

"They take really good care of the dogs there." Paul was making small talk. Did he realize how self-conscious she was feeling?

"Yes, I can't get over the way they've got it furnished, with all those little dog-size love seats and boudoir chairs, and little dining tables and chairs. And all that big open space for them to run around and play in."

"Maybe you should do a story for *Lady Fair* about penthouse-type living for New York dogs."

Now, that was just what Gena needed to get her back to normal. Paul had come onto her turf, and she felt the earth getting steady under her feet.

"It is a good idea, and actually, I've already started on it. And I guess I can thank Wiley—and you. Out of absolutely nowhere I suddenly acquired a dog, and I was lucky enough to meet with your sister, who started me thinking, and you introduced me to East Side Dog Prep and Day Care—if I hadn't the brains to see what a great story it all added up to, I wouldn't deserve to be doing the work I'm doing. I'm working on that story right now. Have been for the last week."

Paul shook his head. "I'm all admiration, Gena. That makes three stories by you I'm looking forward to seeing in *Lady Fair*'s pages."

And as they walked west on Seventy-Ninth Street, she talked about what she'd been learning about a dog's life in New York, and gradually, by the time they reached Fifth Avenue, with the Met museum just ahead of them across the street, she'd lost her self-consciousness. There was a natural rhythm that they fell into together as they walked, and their casual chatter came comfortably, as though they were old friends. She felt as though he could put an arm around her and it would be the most ordinary gesture. Or that she could just as easily put her arm through his.

He looked at his watch. "I haven't had dinner. And I bet you haven't either. Why don't we walk over to the Graydon and get something to eat."

She wondered if the Graydon Hotel was going to become "their" place. It was a seductive idea.

"Seems I'm always starving when I see you. Sure, I could really use dinner. And tonight I have some money, so this one's on me."

Paul's laugh was hearty. "Okay," he said. "I'll let you do that."

"As long as you don't order the steak. I'm not that rich."

"Yes, ma'am. I'll let you eat like a horse. I'll have a dry crust of bread. And some wine. As long as you let me buy the wine."

"It's a deal," she said. And they turned south, and together they walked their dogs to the Graydon Hotel.

* * * *

It was another one of those sweet June evenings, with the coolest of breezes just barely touching the leaves of the trees, and the sun disappearing low across New Jersey, sending some last rays between the buildings and over the park. Gena and Paul were deep in their conversation when someone stopped at their table and a voice said, "Gena?"

She looked up and was amazed to see Sonny Gaile, of all people, and Tim with him, apparently just coming out of the hotel and passing their table on their way out.

Of course! They're here on their honeymoon.

Before she could say a word, Sonny turned to Paul and said, "I didn't know you two knew each other."

Gena turned to look at Paul. "Now who's been eating canaries?" she asked.

Paul was smiling. "The world is full of surprises, isn't it?"

She also remembered, just in time, that they were incognito, and that their wedding was a secret. So she bit her tongue and said only, "It's great to see you guys. What are you doing in New York?"

Sonny and Tim smiled conspiratorially and Tim said, "Catching up on some culture. We like to stay here because it's near the Met."

And Sonny added, with a wink to Paul, "And maybe take care of a little business."

To which Paul merely smiled and said nothing.

Good lord, Gena thought, *people are so full of secrets.*

"Would you like to join us?" Paul asked. "Have you had dinner? We could order another bottle—"

But Tim touched Sonny's arm, as though to remind him they had to be going, and Sonny said, "Can't tonight. But next time. Been great to see you." And as he and Tim headed out to the sidewalk, he said, "Small world, isn't it?"

Now that they were gone, Gena gave Paul a long, questioning look. Paul's response was dismissive.

"I've done some legal work for them."

"You never said."

"I try to not talk about clients."

She was liking this man more and more every minute.

Chapter Twenty-eight

They'd finished their dinner, and they'd finished the bottle of wine. Paul looked at his watch again. "The dog park isn't open yet. Okay with you if we just sit here till nine?"

She thought that was a lovely idea. "Of course," she said.

"Should I order another bottle of wine?"

"Maybe just a glass."

He smiled. "That's probably a good idea."

As he signaled the waiter, she said, "I'm okay, you know."

"I know. You sort of have a glow."

"I guess I'm feeling good tonight."

"Especially tonight?"

"Oh, work has been going well, people are out and about but no one is rushing, a really sweet evening, one of those perfect June evenings we get here in New York. It's as though all the activity just quiets down a little, and you can feel the beginning of summer. I've had a good dinner, I've had a great wine, and I'm feeling good, just being here, in this nice place, with you—"

She stopped, embarrassed.

"I'm glad you said that. And I love that glow you have. Here. With me." She blushed, and he knew it wasn't the wine. He paused while the waiter filled their glasses again, then waited till he was gone. "Gena, when I went to pick up Sweetie Pie tonight, I was hoping I'd see you there. I've been watching for you these last few days, and I was really glad you came in when you did."

He drank a bit of his wine and Gena felt a pounding in her ears. She had some wine, too.

Paul said, "That day at Harriet's, that day she was packing and you came in to get some information about Cresteds, you thought I didn't notice you." The pounding in Gena's ears got a little stronger. "You were wrong. I noticed you the minute you came in. My very first thought was, 'What a good-looking woman!' I figured I'd come and sit with you and Harriet, get in on the session between you, get you know you. But that damned call came just then, and it was too important to put off."

Boom, boom in her ears.

"There was a crisis at the office, and I had to leave immediately."

"I never realized—"

"Of course you didn't. Afterward, I asked Harriet about you, but she was so dithery that day, she couldn't remember a thing, not even your name. I was able to track you down through *Lady Fair*, at least enough to recognize some of your pieces. Harriet reads the magazine regularly, and I've looked through it occasionally. I'd seen the article you did on that old myth about hem lines and the stock market. Whether there's a connection. And your long profile on the French woman who became the head of the International Monetary Fund." He smiled at her. "You're blushing," he said. "That's so sweet."

"It's the wine."

"Of course it is." They both drank a bit more. "When I ran into you on Madison Avenue, only a couple of days later, it seemed like fate—"

"Fate?"

Ding, dong!

"Well, whatever you want to call it. Good luck, at least. And we had the dogs, and a good excuse to keep walking and talking, and I was going to ask you out. But then you said there was a boyfriend, so I backed off."

There was a long, thoughtful silence between them. Gena couldn't take her eyes off him, and he was as intent on her. And the more he studied her face, the more she felt herself going all soft inside.

Her hand was resting on the base of her wine glass. He reached across and placed his hand—that nice hand—over hers.

"Gena, I'm not a man who moves in on another man's girl."

She had the oddest sensation, as though she was melting from the inside out.

"I think I may need another glass of wine for this conversation."

"Oh, no," he laughed. "I'm also not a man who gets a girl drunk so he can have his way with her."

She loved his use of that old-fashioned expression.

"Have your way with me?"

"You know what I mean." Now it was his turn to blush.

"I do. Of course. And I guess there's some code of chivalry that says if I'm some man's girl, then he has dibs on me and no other man can 'move in.' It's an interesting idea."

"Does that bother you?"

She relaxed a little, laughed, and said, "No, not really."

"It's just that there are rules about that sort of thing."

"Why do I get the sense that you're thinking about breaking those rules?"

He looked at her very seriously, as though sizing up how far she'd allow him to go.

"I may be way out of line, Gena, and you'll tell me if I am, but I have a sense, just a sense, that there may be a little trouble between you and the boyfriend. It's not that I want to take advantage of that, but if I'm right, maybe I shouldn't just totally back off." He was quiet for a moment, letting that sink in. Then he said, "Am I right, Gena?"

He waited, and she was silent for a long minute. And another. He watched her very closely.

Finally, she answered him. "I don't know what to say. I'm living with Warren. I've been living with him for several years, and we've been together since we were kids in high school. I wouldn't say it's been perfect, but—" She stopped. She realized she didn't know how to describe how it's been. "I guess we're going through a rough patch right now. And I don't know how it's going to work out. *If* it works out. Lately, we've been not so good together. Maybe it's me. Maybe he's having to deal with some big changes in his future, and it's making him—oh, I don't know—edgy, critical."

"Critical of you?"

"Maybe I don't measure up. The way I used to. Or something." Her gesture was dismissive. "I don't want to talk about it."

She had never seen such deep sympathy on a man's face.

Whatever happens, she thought, *I'll never forget that look.*

There were long pauses now. "Gena, I'm going to put this in your hands. I'm facing a problem, and you're going to decide it for me, one way or the other."

"Maybe I shouldn't have had that last glass of wine. Am I going to need a very clear head for this?"

"Yes." And now he was not joking. "For the last couple of weeks, there's been this offer on the table. The firm wants me to go to Australia, in connection with the work my brother-in-law is setting up there. I thought it would be interesting, a chance to see a part of the world I don't know, spend some time with Harriet and Russ, make some new connections."

"How long?"

"Two months."

Gena felt her heart sink.

"I was planning to accept the offer."

"But what?"

"You know what. I met you." He was dead serious now. "I won't go if you give me a good reason to stay."

"Wow. That's a heavy one."

"I know." He'd put the course of his life in her hands. "You'll want to think about it, of course."

"Funny, my head is perfectly clear now."

He laughed. "It works that way sometimes."

She stared into her empty glass for a while. A long while.

"I want to do the right thing. And the first thing, Paul, is that I really have been thinking about you, too. You're awfully attractive. And I don't just mean you're good-looking. Which, of course, you are."

They both laughed a little, because she was embarrassing him.

"And maybe you'd be a little less attractive if Warren and I weren't having our problems right now. I'll make a confession to you—I've been wondering if cheating on a boyfriend is as bad as cheating on a husband. I guess it is, but still, somehow—"

"I know what you mean. It is just as bad, but somehow—"

"Right. Like, if you haven't made a legal commitment, it's as though you've both been willing to leave certain options open."

"Yep."

"And lately, I've been tempted—"

"With me?"

"I'm not saying. But this choice you've given me…seems sort of unfair."

"It's fair. I'll respect your relationship with Warren if you want me to, and I'll leave you to work it out with him—at least for the next two months. But if you tell me to stay—well, all's fair, as they say, in love and war."

"This isn't love, Paul. This is probably lust. Or at the least, a passing phase, a pleasant distraction. Maybe just a fling."

"Whatever you say." He was smiling.

"You've got that canary look again."

Now he laughed. "I'm usually not a man who takes wild chances. But I'm taking a wild chance now. And I'm willing to see how it works out."

Gena was looking long and hard into her own heart. And when she'd made her decision, she felt as though she was cutting off a part of it.

"You should go, Paul. You should go to Australia, and I should see what Warren and I can work out between us. It's not what I want." She smiled mischievously. "It would be fun to watch two men fight over me." Then she was serious again. "But it's the right thing to do. And either way, whatever happens, no harm done. No serious harm, that is."

Paul's hand was still on hers. "And in the meantime, we're still friends?"

"You bet."

Friends? Oh, if you only knew. You are so attractive, Paul, sitting there, only a table's reach between us, with that nice face of yours and those nice hands. And your intelligence. And you read my pieces!

"We could write to each other, if you like. Or not, if you prefer."

"I guess we could."

"And Gena, they don't have me in chains there. Anytime, if you give me the word, I can be back in New York in a day." He squeezed her hand gently, let it go, and signaled for the check. "And now," he said, "it's after nine. Why don't you and I take the dogs over to the park? And then I'll walk you home. And maybe you'll let me kiss you goodnight."

And they did walk over to the off-leash park, and they sat for a while and talked—like old friends—about what his work in Melbourne would be, and then he walked her home.

And yes, of course she let him kiss her goodnight, in the shadows of some shrubbery that faced the front of her building, away from Alfie and everyone else's eyes, and the kiss she'd expected to be a friendly goodbye was instead a slow and deliberate kiss of such hunger that she knew he needed it to last for at least two months. And before he left, she needed to hold him long enough to memorize his face—and the feel of his body against hers.

* * * *

Warren was watching a movie. "Where've you been?"

"I had to pick up the dog. And then I walked him for a while. In the off-leash park. It's good for him to get the exercise."

Not one word of that was a lie. But she now knew that yes, cheating on a boyfriend was every bit as bad as cheating on a husband—or anyone else. She hated how she felt.

Chapter Twenty-nine

"Oh, Ms. Shaw," Labibbah said. "Mr. Brackman was in real early this morning. He's going to be out of the country for a couple of months, and Sweetie Pie will be here with us till he gets back. And he said that his Sweetie Pie and your Wiley get along so well together, he said if anytime you come by to walk Wiley, like at lunchtime or something, you have his permission to take Sweetie Pie along, too, if you like."

"Well, that was very thoughtful of Mr. Brackman." She handed Wiley over to Labibbah, who set him down onto the floor. "I'll be in a little early this evening to pick him up." She watched him run off to find Sweetie Pie. "Maybe I will take them both for a walk around the block."

As she went out onto the street, she was laughing to herself. "That sly dog," she thought, and she didn't mean the four-footed kind. "He's left her for me, like a memento, so I won't forget him." On her way to the subway entrance, she added, "Not that *that's* likely."

Her agenda for the day included a follow-up call to Grover Simms at Westminster, then an editorial meeting at ten o'clock, and after that, out of the office to do field research at the city's most posh pet accessories shops. That would take the whole afternoon—up to four o'clock, when she'd pick up Wiley. Only a short walk today; she had an after-work agenda, too.

* * * *

It all started with Warren, over breakfast.

"Why am I the one who always has to fry the eggs in this house?"

"What?" She looked up from the *Times*'s food section.

"The eggs. Why do I have to be the one who always fries them?"

"I don't know, Warren. I guess because you've always done them."
She turned a page to follow up on a column about a fancy new Lebanese
restaurant in Midtown.

"I know I always have. That's the trouble. That's something you should
be doing. You don't do any of the cooking around here."

"Warren, no one does any of the cooking around here. Except for
breakfast, we mostly order in or eat out. I'm a rotten cook, you do eggs well.
This is how we've managed the meals for years. What's the problem now?"

"It's not just now. I've been waiting for a long time for you to be more
of the housewife around here. It would be nice, you know. To come home
at night and have dinner on the table."

He was serious, she could see that. And if she'd not been carrying a load
of guilt about Paul, if she hadn't woken that morning thinking of how it
would be to wake up next to Paul, if she hadn't been taking her morning
shower and brushing her teeth and getting dressed with the feeling that
she was walking on very shaky ground, that a big sign hung around her
neck that said, "I've done a bad thing, and I may be about to do an even
worse thing," if it weren't for all of that, she might have handled this latest
complaint of Warren's differently. But what she actually did was to hand
him another stick to beat her with.

"I'm sorry. I really am. I hadn't realized you cared that I never learned
to cook. I just never did, and you seemed to be okay with it." She closed
the newspaper and put it aside. "But I can try. I really can. Tell you what:
I'll leave work a little early tonight, and I'll shop and I'll have a home-
cooked dinner waiting for us when you get home. I really will. If I keep it
simple, I should be able to manage it. Like maybe lamb chops and baked
potatoes and a salad. Would that be okay?"

"Ah, now, that's more like it, baby." Warren sat down at the table and
used a piece of toast to break the yolk of his egg. "Maybe, with a little
practice, you could even be frying the eggs in the morning and have
breakfast ready for us. I'd really love that."

She had an image of herself in an apron, being a little wifey.

This is not going to be easy. But I owe it to Warren to try.

*And I owe it to myself, too—however the future works out—if I'm ever
going to be able to live with myself in peace.*

* * * *

She did the shopping, picked up Wiley and Sweetie Pie, did a quick
walk around the block with them, and was home by five. With help from

Google recipes and the *Good Housekeeping Cookbook* her mother gave her when she graduated from college, she really did have dinner ready when Warren got home. And it was ready without the conventional cliché of the frazzled young housewife's inept and comically frantic disasters. For, after all, how difficult could it be? The oven, pristine until this day, broiled the chops just as it was created to do. It baked the potatoes as though it had been baking potatoes for years. And she kept the salad simple—just some torn-up Romaine lettuce, two sliced-up tomatoes, cucumbers, and scallions, and a bottle of store-bought dressing on the table. She opened a bottle of nice Italian red, and thought about lighting a couple of candles but decided that was going too far. When Warren walked in, it was looking picture-perfect.

"Wow. You really did it. This looks great. I wouldn't mind coming home to this every night." He had his arms around her, hugged her tightly, and said, "I'll go wash up, then let's eat!"

Dinner was fine, and then he went into the living room and turned on the TV and she took care of the cleaning up. Later, in bed, he told her he loved her, he really did. But the truth was, the love-making between them did not make the earth move. It never had, and she had often wondered what that must feel like. No, tonight's love-making, like every other night's, was for Warren's pleasure. Just as tonight's dinner was for Warren's pleasure. Warren had gotten what he wanted, and he was pleased with himself.

Am I only an accessory to his life?

An hour later, in the window niche, with Wiley next to her and a carton of Trio Triple Chocolate ice cream in her lap and the city lights spread out like a carpet of diamonds below her, she peered into her future and tried to think what to do about Warren—and tried very hard not to think about what to do about Paul.

"This is not good, Wiley. I did it the way Warren wanted. All I needed to do was be the way he wanted me to be. And he was really quite nice to me tonight." She pulled Wiley close and whispered into his ear. "He said he loved me. What do you think of that?" Wiley's ear twitched reflexively, but he was silent on the subject. "I should be feeling really nice, shouldn't I?" She looked out into the night for a long time. Slowly, she spooned her way down a quarter of the carton. Then she said, very quietly, "I'm really not feeling very nice at all. The truth is, I'm feeling awful."

"Oh, Wiley." She spoke very quietly into the silent night. "Would it be different with Paul?" She stroked his silky ears and he put his face up against hers, as though they were whispering together. "I shouldn't even

think about that. I owe it to Warren to try. I owe it to all the years we've
been together and whatever it is we've created. I owe it to him to really try."
Then, though she knew she shouldn't, she texted Paul.

> *You slipped out of town like a thief in the night.*
> *I know it's a 21-hour flight, so you're in the air*
> *right now. Have a safe journey.*

She wanted to add, "Love." But she didn't.
An answer came back.

> *Sun coming up over the ocean. Very beautiful.*
> *It's after midnight in New York.*

> *Go to bed.*

And she did.

Chapter Thirty

She was trying hard to concentrate, but it was hard to think about super-expensive and over-the-top accessories for dogs when her personal life was poking her on her arm like a nagging finger, trying to get her attention.

"I know, I know," she wanted to say. "Getting myself sorted out is a lot more important than telling the world about all this stuff." She waved her hand over the materials she'd gathered yesterday afternoon. "Does the world really need to know where they can get a real mink coat for a dog? Or custom-designed, handmade Italian leather boots?" She picked up one of the pictures, then dropped it back down onto the pile. "Here's a dog bed for thirty-four thousand dollars. Does that make any sense? Or this water bowl, gold-encrusted porcelain, for nine hundred and eighty-nine. And an actual diamond dog collar for—*gulp*—$2.3 million? And here's a whole fashion line of track suits and bathrobes and bikini outfits. Gross!"

On the other hand, there were some hand-tailored coats that actually made some sense. She'd already learned that standard pet store coats didn't fit Wiley. His chest was too deep, his back too short and skinny, and his legs much too long. Rain boots that would fit over his long paws would not fasten tightly around his stick-thin ankles. She'd also learned that there is an international cottage industry producing summer and winter wear especially for Chinese Cresteds. Who knew? She planned to do further research to see if there were similar resources for other breeds. And who makes dog beds for Great Danes?

She stared at the pile of photos and notes. She stared at her computer screen. She told herself to focus. She told herself to get to work. But nothing seemed to get her brain in motion.

She simply had to stop thinking that Paul must be in Australia by now, and that it must be afternoon there—well, she couldn't actually figure out what day and time it was in Melbourne, what with crossing the international date line and the big time difference. She knew that it was winter there, but she didn't know what winter in Melbourne would be like. Should he be bundling up in scarves and gloves and a winter coat? Or was Melbourne's winter milder than New York's?

She really wanted to stop thinking about Paul. The whole point of her sending him away was so that she could concentrate on Warren. And even with that thought, a gray cloud of sober reality settled over her like a damp blanket. She deflected it by remembering that she was supposed to be writing an article on ways to outfit a super-rich dog. She wished something—anything—would give her an excuse to leave her desk, take a walk, forget about dogs. Forget about Paul. And Warren. Just check out for a while. Wouldn't it be nice to just sit in the sun and have a glass of wine?

She took a resolutely deep breath and got to work.

That lasted for about two minutes. Her phone pinged with a text message. The caller ID said Sonny Gaile, of all people!

Got a minute?

She texted right back.

For u—anytime. Wassup?

And he answered

I'll call.

The phone rang immediately.

"Great to hear from you, Sonny. You still in town?"

"We're still here, and Tim and I were thinking, what are the chances you can get away for lunch?"

She beamed at her phone.

"Oh, you can't imagine how much I'd like to do that."

"You know a nice place where no one will know us? We're sort of in disguise—hats pulled low and big sunglasses—where we can be left alone and just talk."

"Where are you?"

"I think we're in your neighborhood. Near the World Trade Center. Just walking around, people-watching. Tim bought a scarf from a street vendor and I had a hot dog for breakfast. Mrs. Wilkins would kill me."

"There's a little diner near Rector Street. Nada's Place. It gets busy around one, but I could meet you there for an early lunch—say at eleven thirty?"

"Good. We'll walk around until then."

She gave them the directions and then sat back, smiling. This was just the break she needed this morning. The prospect of a friendly lunch with Sonny and Tim broke the logjam in her head, and suddenly it became easier to write about rich dogs. The first draft was practically all written by the time she needed to leave for the diner on Rector Street.

They were already there when she arrived, tucked away in a corner booth, looking safely unrecognizable.

"You guys having fun?" She was about to say "on your honeymoon," but remembered that the wedding was a secret. "I was so surprised to see you the other night."

"Surprised? We were flabbergasted. Had no idea you knew Paul Brackman."

"And I didn't know you knew him, either. How did that happen?"

Sonny and Tim looked at each other, as though each giving the other permission to talk to her.

"He's been doing our legal work for years," Sonny said. "He did our prenup."

She shook her head and smiled. "So he already knew about the wedding."

"Yep."

"And I was so careful to say nothing about it to him."

"And I bet he was careful to say nothing about it to you."

"Neither one of us knew the other one knew."

"So you're both good at keeping secrets." This was Tim speaking. "I was sure that was true. That's what I told Sonny, didn't I, honey?"

"Yes, you did. That's one reason we picked *Lady Fair* to handle the story. In our business, Gena, everyone needs to be 'on' all the time, performing even when they're not on stage. So it's hard to find people who are 'real' people. But we decided you're a real person. And Paul is, too. In fact," Sonny paused and then said, "you tell her, Tim. You're the one who said it."

"That night, when we saw you together, I said that you and Paul made a good pair. I thought you were a match. We were getting into the taxi, and that's what I said to Sonny. 'Those two ought to get together.' And Sonny said he thought maybe you were together. And I said no, I remembered that you talked about a boyfriend, and his name was not Paul and he wasn't a lawyer, and I think you and the boyfriend are actually living together. And Sonny said, 'Do you think that's working out?' And Gena, it's none of our business, but I had a feeling maybe that match with your boyfriend is not made in heaven, and I'm such a busybody, I just had to butt my nose in where no one has asked for it, and see what's what." Gena was staring at him with very wide eyes. "Have I gone too far?" Tim asked. "You just tell me to buzz off and I will. And we'll have a nice lunch and forget I said anything. But Sonny here thought it would be all right. Because he said he had the same feeling. At the wedding. He said you didn't look happy that day, like something was bothering you. Sonny's real sensitive that way, and I always take whatever he says seriously. Omigod! Gena, honey. You're going to cry! I'm so sorry."

It was true that Gena was on the verge. She grabbed a napkin and dabbed at her eyes and managed to stop the tears that had suddenly welled up.

"You guys are too much," she said. "I thought I was doing a good job of keeping things to myself."

Tim reached a hand across the table and laid it on her arm. Sonny's hand came and rested on hers.

"Would it help to tell us?" Sonny and Tom seemed to speak in sync.

She took a long time to answer their question. Yes, of course it would help. But to talk about it would be to expose herself in ways she never had before, to talk about things she'd never shared with anyone. There they were, Sonny and Tim, two of the most sincere and sympathetic men she'd ever known, waiting for her to decide to trust them. She felt as though she was about to step off a cliff. But maybe, because she held a secret of theirs, it was safe to share one of her own.

"Yes, it would help," she said quietly. Then, with a deep sigh, she went ahead and stepped off the cliff. "Warren's my boyfriend. We've been together for a few years, and lately, well, you're both right. Things haven't been so good between us. I seem to be not so much what he wants anymore. And becoming what he wants may be impossible."

"Why should you become what he wants? You're practically perfect as you are."

"Oh, you guys. I could give you a list. The thing is, I guess I could learn to cook, to be a traditional wife and support him in his work and try to keep him happy no matter how stressful his days become, and help him up the corporate ladder. But there's one thing he really wants more than anything else, and that I can't give him. He wants a woman he can show off to his buddies. To the people he works with. To his boss. He wants to be able to walk into some fancy place and have a gorgeous woman on his arm that everyone will notice." She sighed again and held herself straight, as though to put herself up for their inspection. "And look at me. No way I can be that woman."

Sonny was staring at her as though she'd been speaking Chinese. Tim was resting his chin in his hand and gently shaking his head as though what she was saying was not to be believed.

"What, you guys? What are you thinking?"

"Oh, Gena." This was Tim. "You're breaking my heart. Is this man, Warren, really a man? He sounds like an infant."

But Sonny said, "No. I understand. He matters to you. You care for him. And you want to make it better."

"Thank you, Sonny. That's about it. That's what I'm trying to do."

"And you think you aren't beautiful enough to please him."

She laughed. "Oh, Sonny. I'm not beautiful at all. I'm around truly beautiful women every day, and they're a whole different species. People have been teasing me about my looks for as long as I can remember. In kindergarten, they called me 'Skinny Marink.'"

"I remember that song," Tim said. He thought about it for a moment, dredging it up from the long-ago time when he was five. "I remember, 'I love you in the morning, and in the afternoon, I love you in the evening—' But Gena, that was a little kids' song, all about telling someone you love them."

"I know, but that was the problem. I couldn't get mad, because the song said, 'I love you,' but when they called me that name, it pointed a finger at how I looked. And I was ashamed."

"Don't tell me you're still ashamed."

"It's not just being rail-thin. I wouldn't care, maybe, but all through high school kids had names for me. And it was always the same—not mean, just kidding, friendly even. Warren does it all the time. Like he thinks I'm sharing the joke. How can I be sharing a joke that calls me 'giraffe girl' and 'beanpole' and 'whooping crane'? I laugh and I pretend I don't care, but I just wind up feeling geeky and, well, not lovely. And that's about it."

"And you're in love with this man?" Sonny squeezed her hand.

And Tim said, "He should be horsewhipped." And then, more thoughtfully, he said, "I suppose you've talked to him about it."

"I've tried, but he doesn't get it. He says he's just kidding around, and, you know, like, 'What's the matter? Can't you take a joke?' Like I'm not supposed to mind."

Sonny looked at Tim. "What do you think? Should we go find this guy and beat him up?"

Tim laughed and asked Gena, "How big is this boyfriend of yours? Do you think he could hurt us?"

Gena laughed, too. "He's big." She glanced quickly around to be sure no one could overhear her. "And I can just see the headlines: 'Sonny Gaile and Tim Fine spend their honeymoon in jail.'"

The two men laughed. "Okay," Tim said. "We'll behave."

"But Gena," Sonny said, "your boyfriend's a big bully. If you're determined to stay with him, you at least have to stand up to him."

And Tim added, "You know we're right."

She looked at them fondly. "You guys. A couple of weeks ago we hadn't even met, and now I'm pouring my heart out to you."

"Which reminds me, Gena. We were surprised to see you with Paul. Have you known him long?"

"Only a few days, actually. It was the dogs that brought us together. The two dogs you saw outside the Graydon. The hairless one is mine and the other one, the white one with all the beautiful hair, that's Paul's. Long story."

"Tim noticed them. He said they looked like an interesting pair—one all fluffy and white and the other beige and all skin. They seemed to get along well, didn't they, Tim? And I hope you notice, Gena. Neither one of them seems to notice if the other is pretty enough."

"Right," Tim added. "You think they know something we human beings don't?"

The buzz around them was getting louder and the tables at Nada's were beginning to fill up. The lunchtime crowd was arriving and Gena looked at her watch.

"Well, this has been great, you guys, but it's time for me to get back." She stood up and Sonny and Tim did, too. "Stay," she said. "Have lunch. The moussaka here is to die for. And I'm so glad you called. You don't know how good this has been for me."

There were hugs all around.

"Remember. You have to stand up to bullies."

She put on a brave face. "I'll sure try to."

"And remember, too: Beauty is one of God's mysteries. People who respect that are the best people."

"I'll try."

On the way back to her office, she had a little conversation with herself. "Is Warren actually a bully? That seems a little harsh. A tease, maybe. But he doesn't mean to really hurt me." There was a pause in her internal conversation as she dared to ask herself the question: "Does he? Does Warren actually *mean* to hurt me?" The question hung in the air, unanswerable.

She settled into her chair and brought up the last screen she'd been working on.

"But that was cute of those two, threatening to beat him up. It felt nice, having them rush to my defense like that."

Later that afternoon, she tried to call Warren about dinner plans, but he wasn't answering the phone. She texted him, too, but got nothing back. *Probably in a meeting*, she thought.

With no word from him by the time she headed to Dog Prep to pick up Wiley, she decided it would have to be an order-in night. Linguine Bolognese and a big salad with olives, capers, and garlic bread. Enough for two, but Warren didn't show up until after ten o'clock, and then he said he'd eaten already.

"You could have called."

"Yeah, well, no. I really couldn't. It was pretty intense all day, and we went straight through. Had dinner in the conference room. Pizzas. And coffee all day long—I probably won't be able to sleep tonight. And I'd *better* sleep. I have to be back in the office for a seven-thirty meeting." He was in the bedroom, peeling off his clothes, hanging up his pants and jacket. "I need to settle down. I'm going to take a bath."

"I thought we could talk."

"Talk? What about?" He sat on the bed, taking off his socks.

"Well," she hesitated. "About us. About you and me."

He stopped, looked up at her. "Now? You want to have a talk now? I'm dead tired, I have to be up early. I've got important stuff on my mind and I've got to keep my head clear. Do you think maybe you could have picked a better time?" He stood up and got out of his boxers.

He really does have such a nice body.

"Jesus, Gena! The last thing I need. A little soul-baring heart-to-heart when I'm handling the biggest deal they've ever given me, and you decide this is a good time to talk about 'us.'" He went into the bathroom to start the water running in the tub, and as he closed the door behind him, she heard him add, "Gimme a break!"

Gena sat down on the bed. She imagined Sonny and Tim sitting there with her. Big as life, they seemed. And they were watching her expectantly.

"Maybe," she said to them, "I'll have to find a better time to talk."

Chapter Thirty-one

Bright and early next morning, Ira Garlen popped his head around the door.

"Gena, you busy?"

"Never too busy for you, Ira. What's happening?"

He came into her office and perched on the corner of her desk. As usual, he was dressed in his customary Hawaiian flip-flops, jeans, and chambray shirt, open at the collar, unbuttoned halfway down his chest, and sleeves rolled up.

"Romy deVere called me. She's in town, would like to get together with Marge and me. She has some ideas she wants to propose to *Lady Fair.* Also." He paused and preened a little. "She kind of hinted that maybe I'd like to photograph her. In addition to what we did for your article. Studio shots. And I said, 'Are you kidding?' Can you imagine, Gena? Romy deVere has been photographed by every major photographer of her time—but they got her only when she was young. A chance to show her beauty now, to show the additional depth and experience of all those years. Wow! You bet I said sure. I can't wait. So I spoke to Marge and we're meeting her today at the Auburn Restaurant to set it up."

"Well, good for you, Ira. What a treat."

"You bet. And there's something else, Gena. You must have made quite an impression on her. Romy specifically asked if you could join us. She seems to have taken a fancy to you."

"That's so flattering. I don't know what to say, except, of course, I'll be delighted to join you. Couldn't be a better day for it. It's my birthday today."

"Perfect. We can celebrate. I'll let Marge know. Her office is handling the reservation. She's uptown right now, doing an interview at ABC, but she'll meet us at the Auburn at one o'clock. I'll pick you up and we can go together."

* * * *

They were led through the front room, through the noisy lunchtime clatter of clinking glasses and the animated conversation of New York professionals getting a midday break in their over-pressurized lives, to a separate dining room, a haven of gleaming table linen and equally gleaming flatware, where quiet conversation and, perhaps, more serious deal-making were encouraged. Gena and Ira were the first to arrive. Somehow, Ira had managed to acquire a jacket and tie, and his feet were in loafers. No socks.

They'd barely had a chance to agree that tap water would be fine, and ice water was being poured into their glasses when Marge made an entrance, chic as always, this time in lavender Dior, and taking over the conversation before she'd even sat down.

"What a treat this is. To meet the fabulous Romy deVere. Do you know, my grandfather kept a picture of her in his wallet. He said he'd met her once and she was his fantasy secret mistress ever since. I can't wait to tell her that."

Ira was laughing. "I bet she'll tell you she's heard the same story many times."

"It wouldn't surprise me," Marge said. "And now, I need to run to the ladies' room. Gena, come with me."

Once she had Gena safely behind the closed door, Marge explained why she had to take Gena away from the table. "Just wanted to be sure you know that Ira hasn't yet been let in on the information about Romy's past. We want to be sure it doesn't come out until the story is published."

"That's what I figured. I haven't said anything to him."

"Good girl. Romy mentioned it to me when she called, but I hadn't had a chance to tell you. We'll have to keep the conversation away from your article. If it heads that way, I'll rely on you to help deflect it."

"Okay. I'll do my best."

"Good. Now go entertain Ira while I powder my nose."

Back at the table, Ira was studying the menu. As Gena sat down, he said, "What did Marge want to tell you that I can't hear?"

Gena gave him a sly smile. "Girl talk, Ira."

"Okay, okay. Probably something I'd rather not know."

Gena just smiled and picked up her menu.

Marge was back at the table by the time Romy arrived. She was dressed casually, in a rose-hued cowl sweater and dark, perfectly tailored trousers. Her white hair was loose, but it still fell in the thick, seductive, shoulder-length waves that had been her trademark, and the maître d' recognized her immediately. He brought her to the table with an attitude that could only be described as worshipful.

"Ms. deVere. It is such a pleasure to see you here. Is there anything I can bring you?"

She asked for a dry sherry. His eyes adored her. Clearly, she was accustomed to being adored. She smiled at him. He visibly melted and she held her smile until he was gone. Then she turned that same smile to those at the table. It was wonderful to watch, and Gena enjoyed the whole performance.

* * * *

Mostly, Gena sat quietly while Romy and Ira discussed her wishes and his preferences for the photographs she had in mind.

"It is many years," she said, "since I've had the pleasure of being viewed by a man with a good eye and a mastery of his craft. I've seen your work, Ira, and I would not have selected you to photograph me now, at this time of my life, if I had not seen the depth of your artistry. I believe you will be honest without being unkind." Ira told her he was flattered and honored, and they went on to talk and plan the project while Gena listened and Marge delighted in the great good fortune of bringing these two people together.

And then Ira said, "Gena, Marge tells me the story you did on Romy is coming out in the next issue. It must be really special, to rush it into print so quickly. Tell me more about it."

"Oh, no, Gena!" Romy said. "No, you mustn't. It is bad luck to talk about it before publication." She looked sharply at Ira. "Don't you know that?"

"Not at all," Ira said. "We'd never get our stories out if we didn't discuss them thoroughly beforehand."

"But not *this* story." Romy was imperious. "I am a believer in kismet," she winked at Gena, "and we will not discuss it further." She turned abruptly away from Ira and said to Gena, "When I saw you last, you said your boyfriend was not happy with the dog you found. Have you been able to bring him around?"

Gena could have thought of a hundred topics she'd rather have turned the conversation to. "I'm afraid not. Wiley has to be kept in a separate room when Warren's at home. And at night"—embarrassment colored her cheeks—"well, at night we have to lock him in the kitchen."

"Oh, but that is terrible. That beautiful dog." Romy was outraged. "I will say it though I should not: your boyfriend is a monster."

"Oh, no, Romy. He's not a monster." She wished Romy had chosen a different path to divert Ira's attention.

"Then why do you look so sad when you speak of him? I saw it when you were in Connecticut. I saw it then, I see it now."

"Romy, please. Not here. I can't talk about it here. Not now."

Sonny said Warren is a bully. Now Romy calls him a monster. This is too much.

She felt her eyes filling. She mustn't cry, not here, not at lunch with her editor in chief. What would Marge think of her, and Romy and Ira?

I hate this.

She turned her head away as the first tear fell.

"Oh, my dear," Romy said, placing a hand on Gena's. "We women let men make such a mess of our lives." She gave Ira a brief but disapproving glance.

"Don't look at me," Ira said. "I didn't make her cry."

"Oh, Ira! Do shut up!" This from Marge. And to Gena she said, "I had no idea. How can we help? We've all had just enough wine to be in a very sympathetic mood. Go ahead, Gena. Take advantage of us. Between us, we have tons of IQ points and years of experience and wisdom. Let us help."

That did it. Gena grabbed the napkin, planted her face in it, and let herself have a full minute of really honest misery. Then she pulled herself together, dried her tears, looked up at the others, and saw only simple affection on their faces.

"I'm so embarrassed," she said. "You just caught me completely off guard."

"Gena," Marge said gently, "tell us what's the matter." She looked around the table. "I think we're all good at secrets here." She paused, looking at Ira. "Well, I don't know about you, Ira, but if it goes beyond this table, we'll know who to blame."

"My lips are sealed. But Gena, if you need a shoulder to cry on, who better than a big strong guy like me?"

And Romy said, "If a man is making you unhappy, then there is nothing to do but fix it. Let us help you fix it."

"That's just it. I am trying to fix it. I just don't know if it can be fixed."

They were all looking at her expectantly.

"Oh, it's dumb. Warren and I have been together for years. Since high school. He's a financial analyst at Blass Investments, he's become very ambitious and it looks like he has a really successful future ahead of him."

Now came the hard part. How could she say it? It was so humiliating.

Well, they offered to help. They're ready to help. Who better than these three?

She took a really deep breath.

Jumping out of a plane must feel like this.

Okay, here goes.

"He's beginning to feel I'm not good enough to be with him. He's pretty much said so. Not in quite those words. But he wants me to change. Be more domestic. Pay more attention to him, as though—" she added, with a touch of sarcasm, "as though it would be possible to pay enough attention to Warren. He is definitely self-centered."

"He should do well in the banking world," Ira said drily.

"But I think what he really wants is a prettier woman in his life. He thinks I'm—well, he kind of makes fun of me. He thinks I'm sort of funny looking. I think he'd be happy if I were—well, not like I am. If I were beautiful."

There was silence at the table. Marge and Ira and Romy were staring at her.

She looked at each one in turn.

"What?" She was puzzled. "Why are you looking at me like that?"

Ira said, "Well, right now, it's true. You've been crying. So your face is a mess."

Marge stopped him with a look and then said, "Gena. How long have you been at *Lady Fair?* You must have learned more than that about beauty by now."

And Romy said, "It is a simple matter to make you *look* beautiful. But I think that is not really the problem."

"Yes. I agree," said Marge.

Ira had been studying Gena's face closely. "Of course," he said, "with the right light and the right makeup and hair, it would be easy. I could make you look completely gorgeous in an afternoon."

There was silence around the table, as though Marge and Ira and Romy were all arriving at the same thought.

Then Marge said, "Ira. Are you busy this afternoon?"

"I was just thinking the same thing," Ira said.

And Romy said, "Can I watch?"

And before Gena could quite catch up with what was happening, Marge had paid the check, they'd gathered up all their stuff, taxied themselves back to the *Lady Fair* offices, and whisked her up to Ira's lair on the fourteenth floor, which Ira loved because in New York, many fourteenth floors are really the thirteenth and he found that funny.

* * * *

The call went out to Nell and her crew. Damien, *Lady Fair's* go-to hairstylist, was brought in from his salon. Ira's people were all taken off whatever they were doing and told to hop to it. And from there on, it was a whirlwind of activity and lights and equipment, and changes of clothes, hands wielding makeup brushes, shears clipping at split ends, and eyes peering at her mirror reflection. Ira was running the whole show, with Romy making an occasional quiet suggestion about an accessory or the application of a bit of blush to a cheekbone.

A couple of hours later, he was ready to show Gena the result. He put the photo proofs into her hands and stepped back.

"Well?"

There wasn't a sound from her. She was just staring, silent as a stone, giving each photo careful attention.

Ira's impatience spilled over. "Well!?"

She looked up from the photos. "That's me?"

"No, it's Minnie Mouse. Of course it's you! And very good pictures of you, too, if I must say."

"Ira, I look beautiful. I mean, I look like a beautiful person. You're a genius."

"Well, of course I am. That's what I do. I don't make a woman look beautiful. I show that she *is* beautiful."

She stared at the photos some more, as though maybe she hadn't seen them correctly the first time around.

"I don't understand it, Ira. When I look in the mirror, I see a funny looking woman. All spiky and angular and gawky. And yet, though these are certainly photos of me, you've made what's spiky and angular and gawky look really very lovely. How did you do it?"

"Gena, honey. What comes across as beautiful is not only the magic of lighting and makeup and camera angles. I can show you Oscar winners who are funny looking when they get out of bed in the morning. Of course, there are women who are blessed with perfect features. But perfect features are a dime a dozen. Hollywood is full of them. What you see in film and photo is a combination of what's outside and what's inside, plus some kind of magic. It's truly a mystery. But I think you already know all that." He turned to Romy, who was nodding approvingly. "Ask Romy. She knows."

Romy's smile was both wise and sly. "Yes. Some photographers are magicians. But mostly it is a mystery. Beyond the genius of even the most brilliant photographer." She pointed to the proofs in Gena's hands. "You see there how it happens."

"Yes." She looked at them again. "Is it okay if I keep these?"

"Sure," Ira said. "They're a birthday gift. But you'll get the final prints, too, of course."

"I'm going to treasure these. You have all made this a special day." She hugged Ira and then she hugged Romy. "You don't know how special." Then, as though coming back to earth, she checked her watch. "But I've hardly done a lick of work today and now I have to get back to my office."

As soon as she was gone, Ira said to Romy, "Let's take these up to Marge, see what she thinks."

And when Marge saw them, she said, "Wow! These are wonderful. That girl is absolutely delicious. And she doesn't even have a clue." She studied the photo proofs thoughtfully, and suddenly, Marge came to a conclusion.

"You know what I'd like to do? Let's surprise Gena. You've still got those releases she signed when you were doing the shoot in Connecticut?"

"Of course. Legal has them." A smile was spreading over Ira's face. "If you're thinking what I'm thinking, I think it's a great idea."

"We can move a couple of things around—maybe pull the piece on eyebrow threading, save that for the fall issue. It'll be a quick little behind-the-scenes piece about a hard-working *Lady Fair* features writer. I'll write the copy. If we work quickly, it can just make this next issue before it closes."

"Love it! Great idea."

"It will be *Lady Fair*'s birthday gift to Gena."

"I'm on it right now."

He was gone, and Romy said to Marge, "You are all very kind to this girl."

"I guess she touched a nerve."

"I think the boyfriend is not so good for her."

"I think the boyfriend likes a rigged deck."

"I agree."

"She's going to have to figure it out. It's not her looks. Or her cooking, or her housekeeping. He likes having a woman who feels off balance. It's just a mean bit of sadism. I hate men like that!"

"Yes," Romy said. "I agree. She will have to figure it out herself."

* * * *

They'd planned a birthday dinner with Viv and Dan at Galba's. She was feeling fizzy with excitement and they hadn't even ordered the champagne yet.

"Wait till I show you what *Lady Fair* did for my birthday today." She took the proofs from her bag and handed them first to Warren. "Ira Garlen did this. The man is a genius."

Warren flipped through them, looked really surprised, then laughed and said, "The man *must* be a genius. Look at these, Dan." He handed them on, and to Gena he said, "How did he make you look so good?"

"I—I—guess he—I guess he just—" She was suddenly tongue-tied. This wasn't the reaction she'd expected.

Viv took the pictures from Dan's hand, took a good look at them, and then gave Gena a huge smile. "These are fabulous. You could be a model, Gena." She gave Warren a sharp look and added, "And you, Warren, should appreciate what a beautiful girlfriend you have."

"That's true, Warren," Dan said. "I'm really impressed."

"Yeah. Well, as long as she can carry that photographer around with her all the time. And have someone to do her makeup. You haven't seen her when she gets up in the morning."

"Come on," Viv said. "This is Gena's birthday. Let's play nice."

So Gena's pictures were put away, the subject was dropped, and they pretended not to notice that Warren sulked through the rest of the dinner. When dessert came it was a small cake, and the wait staff and Nick Galba came over and they all joined in and sang "Happy Birthday" to Gena. Warren gave her an obligatory birthday kiss and the waiter took a group picture using Viv's cell phone.

Gena and Warren walked home silently, and when they went into their apartment, Gena took the pictures out of her bag and spread them across the coffee table.

"I think they look nice. I like them. I like how I look."

Warren put his arms around her and said, "I know, baby." His expression was almost sad; it seemed to say he felt sorry for her. "They are nice. They really are. But honey, don't forget, the camera can do wonders. I'm just glad you could see how nice you can look. Maybe that will encourage you to do something about, you know, your makeup, your hair, how you present yourself."

And then he kissed her. It was a long-lasting, serious kiss, and somehow, inexplicably, it seemed to Gena that Warren felt that with that kiss, he was sealing a bargain. She didn't know what her side of the agreement was, but she knew it wasn't the winning side.

She needed to think.

"I'm going to take Wiley out. He hasn't had a proper walk today."

"Don't be long. I have to be up early."

And while she walked Wiley around the block, she shared her thoughts with him.

"Do you think it's possible, when I get back, I'll find that he painted mustaches on my pictures?" Wiley said nothing. "And if he did, I bet he'd expect me to think it was funny."

The pictures were untouched, fortunately, and when she got back to the apartment she put them in a drawer. Warren was already in bed, reading, and when she came to bed, he turned out the light and he made love to her. Afterward, she stared at the ceiling and reviewed the events of the evening.

When she was sure Warren was asleep, she went into the living room with her ice cream, a spoon, and her phone and thought for a while. She ate some ice cream and thought some more, then she ate some more, and then she picked up the phone and texted Paul.

Do u think W. really WANTS me 2 feel bad?

Not just "teasing"???? Not just 4 fun?

Paul's answer came right back.

U bet I do.

In a meeting now. Go 2 bed. I'll text u tmrw

Chapter Thirty-two

She stopped at a Staples on her way from the subway and bought a calendar. Nothing expensive, just an ordinary month-at-a-glance on wire binding. When she got to the office, she cut out the pages for the next two months. She found a space on the wall, right at eye level, got some push pins out of her top desk drawer, and fixed those pages where she could see them easily.

"Two months. That's my deadline. Not such a long time when you're sorting out your life."

And then she got to work. By ten o'clock she was putting together an idea that had been on the back burner of her brain for several months—a piece about the annual Ninth Avenue Food Festival for the spring issue— when Paul's text came through.

Ur on the right track.

It's freezing here.

Wish I were there.

Much to think about.

Bundle up. Stay warm.

Two months, she reminded herself.

But it didn't take two months. Within a few weeks, she'd finally figured it out.

* * * *

It started one evening on the subway. She was heading uptown to pick up Wiley, and some high school kids on their way home from school caught her attention. About sixteen years old, she judged, and she got a kick out of eavesdropping on their adolescent banter, their teasing and kidding and just generally being such *kids*. She was only ten years older now, not even, and already she felt like the "older" generation.

Was I ever that young?

They were two girls and three boys. One of the boys had his arm around one of the girls. The boy was really cute, with curly dark hair and the kind of baby face that would stay cute into his old age. The girl had a plain face and seemed shy and—Gena saw it right away—she was so grateful to have a cute boy paying attention to her. He was telling the others how lucky he was to have a girlfriend who always got good grades, because if she hadn't written his papers for him, he never would have made it through their history class. And Gena thought, *Dummy! If you're so smart, you should know better than to let him get you in trouble.* The girlfriend squirmed a little, with her head down, and she glanced sideways, as though fearful they'd be overheard. But the boy's friends nodded approvingly, told him yes, he really was very lucky, and gave him a couple of light high fives. And the boy squeezed his girlfriend a little closer, kissed her lightly on her cheek and said, "Don't worry, baby. If you get caught, we'll bring you a pizza in jail." And she laughed a nervous little laugh at his joke, and he kissed her again, and her face brightened with an expression that made Gena's heart twist inside her. Gena recognized on that young girl's face the glow of gratitude—because this boy, popular and good-looking, had singled her out for his affection. When the train stopped at Sixty-Eighth Street, the two girls got off. And after the doors closed behind them, Gena heard the cute boy say to his friends, "At least she's good for something." And they all laughed.

Gena heard nothing more for the rest of her ride. She was too stunned. What she'd just witnessed was exactly what Viv and Romy, and her own good sense, had been trying to tell her. She was still in a daze when she came up out of the subway and all the way over to Dog Prep. She collected Wiley, and all the way home to Seventy-Third Street she felt she was going through the five stages of grief. As she came off the elevator and opened the door to the apartment, she had reached anger.

And it was anger that greeted Warren when he arrived about twenty minutes later and saw there was no dinner waiting.

"I thought we had an agreement. I thought you said as long as I let you know when I was getting home, you'd have dinner ready for us." He looked around. "I'm home. I don't see any dinner. What's up?"

"Dinner's going to have to wait tonight. We're going to talk."

"Oh, my God. You starting that again?"

"I'm not starting anything." *But I may be ending something*, she thought. "I'm not starting anything," she repeated, "but you better sit down, Warren, because you're going to have to listen to me."

"Gena, it's been a long day, and I've had to deal with people a lot tougher than you, so don't push me. If you don't want to make dinner, fine, we can order something in. Or we can go out, if you want. Just don't bug me, okay?"

"We're not going out, and we're not ordering in, and we're not having any dinner at all until you've heard what I'm going to tell you. After that, you can do whatever you want."

This was a Gena he didn't know, and he looked at her long and hard. Then he walked over to the bar. "Mind if I have a drink?" He didn't offer to make one for her.

She didn't answer him. She knew the question was rhetorical.

"I heard something on the subway today that reminded me of us ten years ago. High school kids. A girl who is smart enough to know better lets herself be a fool, maybe get herself into serious trouble, just to please a boy. Because he's cute and popular. And she's not."

"And that's why my dinner isn't ready tonight?"

"It's not about dinner."

"What are you telling me, Gena?"

"I'm telling you that I'm not sixteen anymore. I don't know why you always needed to make me feel bad, I don't know what bad thing happened in your childhood, or what gene mutation makes you have to be mean, or some anomaly in your brain, or what there is about the investment banking business that makes you want to hurt me, but hurting me is what you've been doing, and I'm not allowing it anymore."

Warren didn't move. As far as Gena could tell, he didn't react at all. He just stood there silently. He looked her up and down. She watched his face turn very hard and she had the odd sensation that she was seeing a different Warren—whether a new one or the real one, she couldn't tell. It really didn't matter. When he finally spoke, his tone was cool and businesslike.

"Listen honey," he said. "Life is a zero-sum game. For every point a winner wins, a loser loses a point. That's how it works. Now you know."

Everything fell into place. Totally clear.

"I get it, Warren. In other words, you need someone, anyone—might as well be me—to be less so that you can be more. That's what made you pick me, way back then, when we were kids in high school. With me, you could always feel like a winner—because teasing me made me feel bad and that made you feel good. Warren, that's so sick! You could always say you were just joking, and I could always tell myself it was all in fun, because I was so sure I was lucky to have you. A little teasing was a small price to pay. But it's not a small price—and Warren, it's no longer teasing. You're not telling me I'm a cute sort of gawky string bean. You're telling me I'm not good enough for you. Not good enough for a man who means to be important. Do you honestly think I can let myself be that person for you? The person who loses so that you can win? No, Warren. I'm not that person. Not anymore."

Warren continued to look her over carefully. Sizing her up, like she was a piece of furniture he was considering buying. Or not. He went to the bar and set his empty glass on it. He didn't fill it again. He turned and said it very simply.

"Then maybe it's time for us to split up."

"I think that's what you wanted all these months, isn't it?"

"I want what's good for me. And you're not good for me anymore, Gena."

She was astonished. That should have hurt. But it didn't. Not at all. The simple clarity of it, for both of them, made everything easy.

"I'll go stay in a hotel tonight," Warren said. "You'll need to pack up your things. Take a couple of days if you need to."

"No," she said. "The apartment is yours. You stay here tonight. I'll come back tomorrow afternoon, while you're at work, and arrange to get my things out. There isn't much. My clothes, a few books, some jewelry—it can all be stored till I get settled. I'll leave the keys tomorrow."

She picked up Wiley, who had been at her feet the whole time.

"You'll be glad to see the end of him, I know."

Warren laughed. "You got that right."

At the door, she stopped, thinking. "Warren, just tell me: all those days away from home, all those golf dates and tennis games, all those nights home late—is there another woman?"

Warren's look was almost pitying. But before he could answer, Gena said, "Never mind. It really doesn't matter."

And she walked out. And she didn't cry a single tear.

* * * *

The Graydon Hotel was dog friendly, and she already had some feeling for it, so she decided to check in. She'd considered asking Viv, but Viv would want to hear a full replay, and she really didn't feel like talking. Her life had just taken a major turn, and she needed to think. No, actually, she needed to *savor* what she had just done. She was feeling lightheaded and happy. She checked in, parked Wiley in the room, all comfy on the big bed, and went into the restaurant. She ordered a steak and potatoes and salad and brussels sprouts and red wine and chocolate cake and ice cream, and she felt like a free woman!

God! she thought. *Life is good!*

While she waited for the steak, she got her phone out of her bag.

"Paul will be home in about four weeks," she said to herself. "We'll see what happens then."

I finally figured it out. Will explain when I see u.

No answer came back, but he was probably in a meeting.

Chapter Thirty-three

She was in Marge's office first thing in the morning. "I need to talk to you," she said.

"And I need to talk to you, too," said Marge. "But you go first."

"I'm going to need a little time off this afternoon."

"No problem. What's up?"

"You'll be glad to know it's all over between Warren and me. I moved out. I need to get my stuff out of his place."

"You don't seem unhappy about it."

"I'm not unhappy. And I want to thank you. You helped. Nothing to talk about now. Just wanted to let you know."

"Okay. I'm glad. Do you have a place to stay?"

"Not yet. I'll be at the Graydon Hotel until I work things out."

"Well, frankly, Gena, for a woman who just ended a long-term relationship, you're looking wonderfully chipper."

Marge picked up a pen and made a note on a pad. "Tell you what," she said. "Take off a couple of days. Today's Thursday. Take a long weekend. We can spare you till next Tuesday. You'll need some time to get your things organized, find a new place, and so on."

Gena was about to speak, but Marge waved her off. She paused and tapped her pen on the desk a couple of times, thinking. Then she apparently made a decision. She smiled and said, "I was going to wait till next week, but this is a better time to tell you."

Gena stayed silent.

"With Dinah gone, we need a new features chief. I've been so impressed by the work you've done, I'm making you Dinah's replacement. I was going to make the announcement next week, so let's keep it quiet till then. But in the midst of your current upheaval, I think you can use a little extra time to get used to your new title."

She sat back and enjoyed the look on Gena's face.

"Flabbergasted" was probably the right word for it.

"I don't know what to say. I'm—I'm—I'm speechless."

"Well, don't stay that way, because you're going to have to make a little acceptance speech."

"Marge, this is too much. I mean, thank you. Thank you, of course. In a million years, I couldn't have expected—"

"Now, now. Save it for the announcement."

Gena closed her mouth abruptly.

"One last thing, Gena," Marge said, "and then you've got to go, because I have a busy day." Gena could see Marge visibly move into a higher gear. "The next issue of *Lady Fair* will be out tomorrow, and we put two of your stories in this month's issue. The Sonny Gaile wedding couldn't wait. That story is bound to be out soon, whether we break it or someone else does. Be prepared to deal with some press on that one. And the Romy deVere story is just too good to wait, so we went with that one, too. And God knows what the reaction to that will be, so brace yourself." She put down the pen and Gena realized they were finished. "Now go," Marge said. "Enjoy your little vacation. And good luck with your new status. Boyfriend-free. Yay for you."

As Gena reached the door, Marge remembered. "Oh, yes. There's something else. I almost forgot. When you get your issue of the magazine, look on page eighty-seven. Just a little something I think will interest you."

Gena paused in the doorway.

"Marge. I just want to say I—"

"Go!"

Gena closed the door behind her.

Chapter Thirty-four

She let herself into the silent apartment and walked through it knowing this would be the last time she'd see it. She'd arranged for moving people to come and pack up her things—as she'd told Warren, just her clothes, some jewelry, books. Not much. The movers were already downstairs, making arrangements to use the service elevator. When they arrived, she was amazed to see how quickly her things were boxed up and gone. She'd kept separate what she'd need until she got settled, and had those things packed in a suitcase. She looked around one last time, realized she would miss nothing at all, breathed one sad sigh, put the keys on the little table near the door, and left.

She'd taken Wiley to Dog Prep, where he would stay till tomorrow, so once her things were moved, she had the day totally free. Free to think about her future, free to recognize the major promotion Marge had given her, free to think how that might change her life. With all that freedom, she did a really extraordinary thing: she went to a movie.

It was probably the first time in her life she went to a movie by herself. It was a remarkably freeing experience. She was discovering, for the first time, that her life—her precious life—really was her own. When she came out of the movie, she took a walk. She walked in the park. Glorious Central Park! Glorious in its early evening languor. Glorious because this, too, was all hers. The whole world was hers. She was in heaven.

She went back to the hotel. As she walked through the lobby, she remembered she'd been so preoccupied she forgot to pick up her copy of *Lady Fair* at the office, so she bought a copy at the gift shop. She started to leaf through it and saw the Romy deVere story.

"Omigod!" There was Wiley, face to face with the gorgeous Romy, perfect profiles facing each other across the page, perfectly imperious, perfectly god-like, both of them perfectly marvelous. "Wait till I show him," she said. "No one can possibly call this dog ugly! Look how incredibly beautiful he is!"

She got herself comfortably settled into the corner of one of the big lobby sofas, eager to see what the finished product looked like. She was deep into the story and was feeling very proud of herself.

"It's a really good story, Gena. I read it on the plane."

She didn't look up. But she knew that voice.

He sat down beside her.

"Mind if I join you?" he said.

She kept looking down at the magazine in her lap as though she would take no notice, but she was struggling to control the smile that was trying to break out.

"I thought you were in Australia." She kept looking down.

"I was. But I saw your text message."

"I didn't tell you to come home."

"Are you sorry?"

She turned to him quickly. "Oh, no! Oh, Paul, no! I'm so glad. But how did you know?"

"I know how to read between the lines. You were ready."

"I am ready. Oh, yes, I'm so ready. And I have so much to tell you. But how did you know I'd be here?"

"I didn't. My place is all locked up, dust covers over everything, so I planned to stay here till the apartment's ready. I was just going to check in and I saw you sitting here. What are you doing here?"

"Long story. I'm staying here, too."

"Does that mean you and Warren—"

She smiled. She nodded yes. "I escaped," she said.

There was barely a beat while he took that in. When he spoke, his eyes were locked on hers. "Does that mean I get to take you to bed?"

She felt her heart go thump. "Oh, Paul. I'm so glad you're here."

"We're in a public place. I can't kiss you here."

"You can kiss me."

"Not the way I want to."

She was having trouble breathing. She had never seen such hunger in a man's face before. Not like this. Never for her. She could barely speak.

"My room or yours?" Her face was close to his.

"I haven't checked in yet,"

"Then for God's sake," she whispered, "let's get up to mine!"

* * * *

Hours later, they were two exhausted, sweaty bodies, lying naked, entwined among tangled sheets.

"I'm starving," she said.

"Me, too. I haven't eaten since San Francisco." He reached across her to the phone on the nightstand. "I'll call room service. What'll it be? Steak? Fries?"

She nodded, smiling.

He ordered steak and fries for both of them. Plus wine. And lots of ice cream. Chocolate ice cream.

She had his free hand in hers and held it to her face, loving the strong feel of it, warm against her skin.

"You have great hands," she said. "I think your hands were the first thing I fell in love with."

He held her face in both his hands, as though they contained a precious object. "And I fell in love with this face, the first moment I saw it at my sister's place."

"Oh, come on, Paul. That's a bit much."

"Gena. What would it take to make you see yourself as you should? I would have thought those photos by Ira Garlen would have done it."

"How did you see those photos? I have them packed away."

He looked at her kind of funny. He got out of bed and dug the magazine out of the tumble of clothes on the floor.

"Here," he said, riffling through the pages. "Here, on page eighty-seven."

That rang a bell. Marge had told her to look at page eighty-seven. And there they were, Ira's glamour shots of herself. Gena Shaw, looking gorgeous. Gorgeous in her own eyes, because she was seeing herself through Paul's eyes.

And she saw that she was beautiful. And she began to cry.

And Paul held her close and said, "Don't cry, Gena. Everything's going to be all right now." And he put his nice hands around her and pulled her close.

And from then on, everything was all right.

Epilogue

One month later

Paul's summer house in Maine was perfect. Isolated on a long stretch of the Atlantic shoreline, it was big and sunny, with tall windows and a sliding door that opened onto a broad deck that faced the ocean and ran the whole length of the house. Early afternoon, and Gena and Paul were on the deck, stretched out on lounge chairs. The sun was hot, the breeze off the water was cool, and the Schloss Johannisberg Riesling was perfectly chilled. Wiley and Sweetie Pie were snuggled up against Gena, who had the latest issue of *Lady Fair* open across her lap.

"Look, you guys. Look here." She held the magazine up so the dogs could see their pictures. "See? That's you, Wiley." Pointing to his picture. "See? And Sweetie Pie, here's you." The dogs studied their pictures. "This is my article about dogs in New York. Six pages. With lots of pictures. See? And you two are the main ones. So now you're famous!" Both dogs looked mildly interested, wagged their tails, and then curled up again, close to each other and close to Gena.

"A lot they care." Gena was laughing. "I guess they don't appreciate what it means to be featured in *Lady Fair.*"

"They wear their fame lightly. Smart animals." Paul leaned over and put a kiss on Gena's cheek. "Harriet called this morning. She saw Sweetie Pie's picture in this issue and she's so excited."

"I owe your sister a big thank you—for bringing us together."

"I'll let her know." He paused. He looked out to sea for a long minute. Then he said, "I have some other news for you."

"Yes?"

"News about your ex-boyfriend."

"Warren?"

"Yep."

"You're looking funny. Like—you know—that canary." His expression was an odd combination of pleased and serious, like he was going to drop a big secret bomb. "Okay," she said. "Tell me."

"It's a good thing you broke up with him when you did."

"Yes?"

"Well, it's not public yet, but I've got it from people I know at Blass Investments, and I can tell you, because the media has it now and it'll be in the papers in a day or two." He took a long sip of his wine while he thought about how to break the news. "The thing is, Gena, your ex-boyfriend has got himself into some real trouble." Again, he paused. Then he said, "But first, I'm sorry I have to tell you this part, but it seems Warren had been messing around with some woman, and I'm afraid it goes back maybe as much as a year." He reached out a hand and took hers. "I know, darling. And I'm sorry."

She wasn't prepared to hear it, but it really wasn't a surprise to learn that Warren was a snake. Still, she knew she'd need some time to deal with just how reptilian he'd actually been. Some time, yes—maybe several days. But not now. She took a deep breath, lifted her head bravely, and braced herself.

"Paul, I know you're not telling me this just to spread some gossip. What's the rest of the story?"

"Well, this woman just happened to be working at Isler Global Enterprises, a secretary or something, and your boyfriend was working on a major Blass Investments project, putting together a big financing deal for Isler. Seems this woman sucked him into some criminal scheme involving insider trading on Isler stock, and the two of them expected to split some big bucks. But they weren't as smart as they thought they were; the SEC had been tracking them for months. And now it looks like your ex-boyfriend and his new girlfriend are going to jail."

"Gee," Gena said. She sipped her wine. She'd expected Paul's news to be painful, and she was surprised that she felt so calm. "So it's good I left him when I did."

"I guess."

"I feel a little sorry for him."

"That's natural."

"But not much."

Paul laughed. "You'll get over it," he said.

"I know."

"You could visit him in jail."

She laughed, too. "I don't think I will."

Paul leaned over and kissed her. "So you escaped?"

"Totally. And now I'm safe."

"Yes, you are," Paul said. "Totally safe."

And he kissed her again.

ABOUT THE AUTHOR

Joan Myra Bronston grew up in New York City, married her college sweetheart, and went with him to Germany for a year while he was in the Army and where she worked as a telex operator and mail clerk. They then moved to Austria, where Joan spent five years teaching at an international school. She is the mother of three wonderful girls and the grandmother of a super-wonderful grandson. Joan was also a secretary, social investigator, and psychiatric researcher before entering law school and eventually becoming a corporate attorney. In addition to her years in Europe, Joan has lived in Pittsburgh, Chicago, and, for eighteen years, Salt Lake City. At last, she has closed the circle and returned to her first and most beloved—New York City. Visit her website at jmbronston.com, find her on Facebook, and follow her on Twitter @JMBronston.

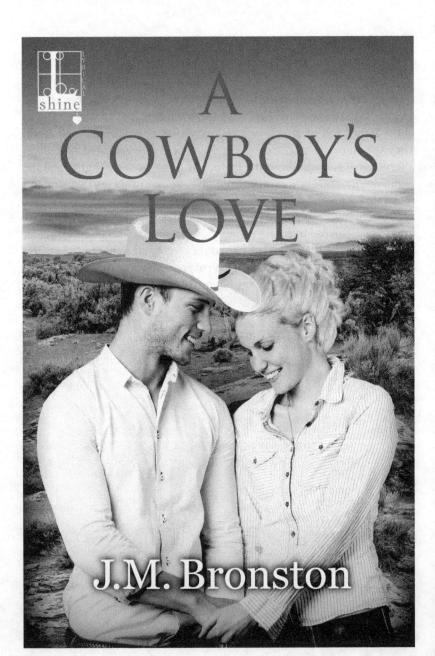

A
COWBOY'S
LOVE

J.M. Bronston

Summer on the Cape

J.M. Bronston

Printed in the United States
by Baker & Taylor Publisher Services